A
TOR
DOUBLE
ACTION
WESTERN

**Look for Tor Double Action Westerns
Coming soon from these authors**

MAX BRAND
ZANE GREY
LEWIS B. PATTEN
WAYNE D. OVERHOLSER
FRANK BONHAM
STEVE FRAZEE
WILL HENRY
CLAY FISHER
HARRY SINCLAIR DRAGO
JOHN PRESCOTT

Zane Grey

AVALANCHE

THE KIDNAPPING OF ROSETA UVALDO

TOR®

A TOM DOHERTY ASSOCIATES BOOK
NEW YORK

AVALANCHE

Copyright 1928 by *Country Gentleman*, Curtis Publishing Co.; copyright renewed 1956 by Romer Grey, Loren Grey, and Betty Zane Grosso.

THE KIDNAPPING OF ROSETA UVALDO

Copyright 1929 by *Ladies Home Journal*, Curtis Publishing Co.; copyright renewed 1957 by Romer Grey, Loren Grey, and Betty Zane Grosso.

A TOR Book
Published by Tom Doherty Associates, Inc.
49 West 24 Street
New York, NY 10010

Cover art by Faba

ISBN: 0-812-50529-8   Can. ISBN: 0-812-50530-1

First Edition: March 1990

Printed in the United States of America

0 9 8 7 6 5 4 3 2 1

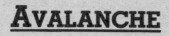 Avalanche

1

Not many years after General Crook drove out the last wild remnant of the Apache Indian tribe, the old Apache trail from the Mogollons across the Tonto Basin to the Four Peaks country had become a wagon road for the pioneer cattlemen and sheepmen who were drifting into the country.

Jacob Dunton and his family made camp one day at the crossing of the Verde. The country began to have a captivating look for this Kansas farmer. From the rim top his keen eyes had sighted a brook meandering through grassy clearings in the dark green forest below. His wife Jane and Jake, their six-year-old boy, were tired from the long journey, and a few days' rest would be good for them. While they recuperated in camp Jacob rode up toward the rim, finding the magnificent forest, the deep canyons and grassy swales, the abundance of game, much to his liking.

Upon his return one day he found Jake playing with a handsome, curly-haired lad, perhaps a year older than himself.

"Hullo, whose kid is thet?" he asked his pioneer wife, who was still young, buxom, and comely.

"I don't know," she replied anxiously. "There have been several wagon trains passing by today. They stopped, of course, for water."

"Reckon this boy got lost an' hasn't been missed yet," replied Dunton. "There'll be someone ridin' back for him."

But no inquiring rider visited the Dunton camp that day, nor the next, nor the day following.

"Jake, what's your new pard's name?" Dunton had inquired of his son.

"I dunno. He won't tell," replied Jake. Name obviously did not matter to this youngster. He was too happy with his playmate to care about superficials.

Mrs. Dunton managed to elicit from the

lost boy the name Dodge, but she could not be sure whether that was a family name or one belonging to a place. The lad was exceedingly shy and strange. A most singular thing appeared to be his fear of grown people.

Dunton had decided to homestead in a beautiful valley up the creek, yet he was in no hurry to move. By the wagon trains and travelers who passed his campground he sent on word of the lost boy, Dodge. No one, however, returned to claim him.

"Jane, I've a hunch his people, if he had any, don't want him back," said Dunton seriously to his wife one day.

"Oh, no! Not such a pretty, dear little boy!" she remonstrated.

"Wal, you can never tell. Mebbe he didn't have no folks. I don't know just what to do about it. I cain't go travelin' all over the country lookin' for a lost boy's people. It's gettin' time for me to locate an' run up a cabin."

"We can keep him until somebody does come after him," said Jane. "He an' Jake sure have cottoned to each other. An' you know our Jake was always a stand-offish boy."

"Suits me," replied the pioneer, and forthwith he fashioned a rude sign upon which he cut the words LOST BOY, and an arrow pointing up the creek. This he nailed upon a tree close to where the creek crossed the road. With this duty accomplished he addressed himself to the arduous task of getting his family and outfit up to the site he had chosen for a homestead.

Little Jake called his new playmate Verde, and the name stuck. No anxious father came to claim Verde. In time, and for long after the rude sign had rotted away, the crossing by the road was known as Lost Boy Ford.

The years passed. Ranches began to dot the vast, timbered Tonto Basin, though relatively few in number, owing to the widely scattered bits of arable land with available water. A few settlements, even far more widely separated, sprang up in advantageous places. Wagon trains ceased to roll down over the purple rim and on down through the endless forest to the open country beyond the ranges. The pioneers from the Middle West came no more.

The Tonto remained almost as isolated as before its domain had been invaded. In one way it was as wild as ever it had been in the heyday of Geronimo and his fierce

Apaches; and this was because of the rustler bands that found a rendezvous in the almost inaccessible canyons under the rim. They preyed upon the cattlemen and sheepmen, who would have waxed prosperous but for their depredations. Jacob Dunton was one of the ranchers who was kept poor by these cattle-stealing marauders. But despite his losses he could see that the day of the rustler was waning. In fact, the tragic Pleasant Valley War, which was heralded throughout the West as a battle between cattlemen and sheepmen, was really between the ranchers and the rustlers, and it forever broke the stranglehold of the livestock thieves. Slowly the Tonto began to recover, and it began to hold promise for the far future.

Jake and Verde were raised together in a log cabin that nestled under the towering gold and yellow craggy rim. The brook that passed their home roared in spring with the melting snows and sang musically all during the other seasons.

The boys grew up with the deer and the bear and the wild turkeys which ranged their pasture land with the calves and colts. They learned how to track animals as other boys learned to play games. It was to be part of their lives. They hunted and trapped before they even knew how to read. In fact, the few summers' schooling they managed to get did not come until they were between twelve and sixteen years old.

Both of them grew into the rangy, long-limbed type peculiar to the region. The Tonto type was a composite of rider and hunter, wood chopper and calf brander, with perhaps more of the backwoods stamp than that of the range.

Jake, at twenty-two, was a lithe, narrow-hipped, wide-shouldered young giant, six feet tall, with as rugged and homely a face as the bark of one of the pines under which he had grown to manhood. He had a mat of course hair, beetling brows, a huge nose, and a wide mouth. But his eyes, if closely looked into, made up for his other possible defects. They were clear gray, intent and piercing, even beautiful in their latent light.

Verde, at twenty-three, was a couple of inches shorter than Jake, a little heavier, yet of the same supple, lithe build, fair and curly-haired, ruddy-cheeked, with eyes of flashing blue, handsome as a young woodland god.

And these two, from the day of their strange meeting at Lost Boy Ford to the years of their manhood, had been inseparable. No real blood brothers could have been closer.

Jake liked hunting best of all work or play, while Verde inclined to horses. Being a born horseman, naturally he gravitated toward riding the range. Jake was the more proficient with rifle and six-shooter, as he was also with everything pertaining to trapping wild animals. Verde had no peer in the use of a lasso. He could rope and throw and tie a steer in record time. Jake's father called Verde the champion "bulldogger" of the Tonto. Verde was not so good with an ax as Jake, but he could mow his way down a field of sorghum far ahead of Jake.

Thus the two of them, with their opposite tastes and abilities, made a team for Jacob Dunton that could not have been equaled in all the Tonto Basin. Long ago Dunton had abandoned any hope of ever learning Verde's parentage. In fact, he did not want to. Verde was as his own son. And Verde had all but forgotten the mystery behind his boyhood. The Duntons had no other children; and the great herd of cattle they hoped to amass someday would belong equally to Jake and Verde.

In spring, after the roundup, which was a long arduous task, owing to the wild

timberland and rough canyons where the
cattle ranged, there would be the plowing
and the planting, the clearing of more
land, the building of fences. In the fall
would come the harvesting, which time,
of all seasons, these backwoods pioneers
loved best. They had their husking bees
and bean-picking parties and sorghum-
cutting rivalries—and their dances, which
were the very heart of their lives. In late
fall they killed pigs and beeves and deer
for their winter meat; and from then on
to spring again they chopped wood and
toasted their shins before the open fireplace.

During the autumn the settler families
on the upper slope of this Tonto Basin
gathered once a week for a dance. Occa-
sionally it was held at a ranch cabin, sometimes in the woodland schoolhouse, but
mostly in the little town of Tonto Flat.

The dance represented their main so-
cial life. They had no church, no county
house, no place where old and young
could meet. Therefore the dance consti-
tuted a most serious and important affair.
It was here that the strapping young
backwoodsmen met and won their sweet-
hearts. In fact, that was perhaps the vital
purpose of the dances. There was little
other opportunity for courting.

And seldom did a dance occur without one or more fights, one of which, now and then, could be serious. Fighting was characteristic of the Tonto youths. Had not their fathers fought the rustlers for twenty years? And as these hardy pioneers had settled many feuds over cattle, sheep, land, and water with cold steel or hot lead, so their sons settled many rivalries with brawn and blood.

Jake and Verde went to all the dances. Even when off on a hunt up into the canyons or over the rim, they made sure to get back in time for the great event of the week. And Jake and Verde were very popular among the valley girls. Seldom did they take the same girl twice in one season, and every occasion was a gala one. Sometimes they exchanged girls—an event which was regarded with wonder and amusement by their young comrades, and always with concern by their elders. Jake and Verde were not responding satisfactorily to the real purpose of the dance. Neither youth evinced any abiding interest in any one girl. They were both capital catches for any young woman, and this, coupled with their debonair indifference and their boyish brotherly absorption in each other, was the cause of considerable pique.

"Wal," said Jacob Dunton, "I reckon them thar boys of mine ain't feelin' thar oats yet."

"I'm tellin' you, Pa," replied his wife, "it ain't that. They're both full of fire an' go. It's jist that Jake an' Verde are too wrapped up in each other to see any of these steady home-makin' lasses they meet. I love Jake an' Verde jist as they are, but sometimes it worries me."

"Reckon thar's reason for consarn," said Dunton, shaking his shaggy head. "Some hussy will split them like a wedge in dry pine someday."

2

ONE NIGHT, AT TONTO FLAT, AN EXTRA DANCE was given in honor of Miss Kitty Mains, a newcomer to the settlement.

Jake and Verde, learning the news late, arrived without partners when the dance was in full swing. They had ample time to see Miss Mains and watch her before there came any opportunity to meet her. And so even before this meeting took place the havoc had already been wrought.

They also had plenty of time to learn all about her; the information was voluntarily offered by swains as dazzled as they. Kitty was the daughter of a St. Louis horse dealer, who had come to Arizona for his health and who was going to buy out the Stillwell cattle interests and take up ranching on rather a large scale. He was reputed to be rich.

But this news would not have been necessary to excite interest in Kitty Mains. She was strikingly beautiful and something quite new to the gallants of the Tonto Basin. She was small of stature, though graceful and well rounded of form. She had a face that struck men and women alike as pretty and pert, and then gradually grew on one. Her hair was brown, curly, luxuriant, and rebellious. Her small lips, usually curved in a smile, were of the color and sweetness of a ripe cherry. She had a complexion that made the tanned and ruddy skin of the Tonto girls look coarse by comparison. She had an additional advantage over them by being daintily and stylishly dressed, her Eastern gowns showing something of her pretty round arms and white neck. But Kitty's superlative charm lay in her eyes—in the remarkable fact of their variance, for one was blue and the other hazel—and of their strangely contrasting beauty. As it was undoubtedly a fact that Kitty Mains could look at a youth with different kinds of eyes, so it seemed that she could look with two kinds of natures, one sweet, wistful, appealing, and the other a dancing devil.

There was not the slightest doubt that she had heard all about Jake and Verde before they were introduced to her; and very little doubt of her curious and divided interest. No good angel was hovering near these raw and impressionable young men to warn them that Kitty Mains was an unconscious and instinctive flirt, an insatiably greedy little soul who lived on love and had never yet returned it, whose nature would never allow her to brook such a beautiful bond of brotherly affection such as that which long had bound Jake and Verde so closely together. She had the animal instinct that either garners for herself or destroys.

Out of her multiplicity of partners she found several whom she could exchange or desert for Jake and Verde. So in time they got to dance with her. The others girls present already knew, if Jake and Verde did not know, what had happened.

Kitty was as different to each as were her two eyes and two natures. Verde she tormented with that dancing little demon, tantalizing him, courting him with a running challenge of talk wholly new to him and utterly irresistible, always escaping from his eager arm yet continually drawing him on. Jake she entwined as if she were a clinging vine. She had little to say to this quiet, lonely, backwoods boy. But she gave him that shy, sweet, wistful blue eye, and yielded her soft form to the dance, so that her fragrant hair brushed his lips.

Jake and Verde left the dance in the gray hours of the morning, only when there seemed no more hope to get another dance with Kitty. They rode out under the dark blue dome of sky with its mantle of white stars. They did not feel the nipping, frosty air. They raved and babbled like two silly lads over the charms of the new girl; and always ended with praising the two different eyes—the blue and the hazel—that were so sweet, so strange, so beautiful.

They rode off the highway into the trail through the lonely forest, under the dark pines, and still they talked on, raving over the charms of the new girl from St. Louis, each trying to outdo the other in the extravagance of his praises. But at last they fell silent.

Deeper and higher into the forest land they rode, while the first flush of dawn changed the steely sky to rose over the dark-fringed canyon rim under which they lived. The rose turned to gold, and burst into the rising glory of the sun.

It was like the thing that had as suddenly burst in their own hearts.

All this happened to Jake and Verde along about the end of September, just at the beginning of the golden autumn season.

At first they found time to ride into Tonto Flat together. Then Jake made an excuse to go alone one day, while Verde was off somewhere on the range. When the next dance came around, it was Jake who was the proud escort of Kitty Mains.

Verde did not know what to make of the matter, particularly of his conflicting emotions. It hurt that Jake had not confided in him for the first time in his life. He went to the dance alone, silent and troubled. Kitty gave him more dances than she had reserved for Jake. This was contrary to the custom of the backwoods, for the escort always looked after his partner's dances, and took them all himself if he chose. Jake would have been generous, but he was not permitted to choose, and he found himself lucky to get the few she deigned to give him. Thus it was that Jake had the honor of escorting this captivating and willful damsel, but

Verde received most of her dances and the most dazzling of her smiles.

The next week the first rift appeared in the perfect relationship that had existed so long between these more than brothers. They did not yet understand what was taking place. But they did not ride together, nor work, nor hunt together. Verde was gone from home for two days, and returned by way of Tonto Flat, obviously with good reason to be exultant. And it was he who took the bewildering Miss Kitty to the next dance, where his triumph was all too short-lived, for he had to suffer the same treatment she had accorded Jake on the previous occasion.

This triangle affair had now become the talk of the Tonto Basin. Never had the dances been so largely attended; and a girl would have had to be vain indeed not to be satisfied with Kitty Main's conquest of the Dunton boys.

They neglected their fall work to such an extent that Dunton took them to task. But his unfamiliar and rude criticism only acted like burning embers upon naked flesh. Mrs. Dunton was too wise to say anything, but she grew more troubled as the days passed. The young men of the Tonto awaited with keen zest and wild speculation the inevitable fight. The young women, aside from natural jealousy and resentment, did not enjoy the strained situation.

Two more dances, one of which Kitty did not attend at all, leaving it a total loss for the lovesick twain, and the other to which she went with young Stillwell, brought matters to a climax between Jake and Verde.

They grew estranged, a feeling which found expression in a desire to be alone rather than in an open break. Their very avoidance of each other's company widened the spiritual gulf that grew wider between them. Because of their long and beautiful companionship, anyone might have imagined that they would talk the matter over in a frank, manly way and decide to go to Kitty together and make her choose between them. But the very intensity of their feelings precluded that. They were in the grip of something beyond their experience.

Everything in the Tonto, according to the old backwoodsmen, presaged one of the long, lingering, late falls. These Indian summer seasons were welcomed by the pioneers. They made preparation for winter less arduous and meant that the winter would be shorter. But sometimes a late fall would end with a terrific storm, and that was always bad. Severe storms up under the rim were liable to destroy much of the improvement accomplished during the summer, not to mention the loss of stock.

The hard frosts did not come; the rains held off; the leaves changed color so slowly that the wonderful golden and scarlet and purple blaze of the canyons did not arrive at its fullness of beauty and fire until toward the end of October. The wild denizens of the forest gave no signs of the approach of winter. Ordinarily the deer and turkeys would be down off the mountain; the acorns would be ripe; the trails would be colorful with fallen leaves; the bears would be fat and "located," as old Dunton would call it. Over all the wilderness lay a drowsy, slumberous sense of waiting. A deep sighing breath soughed through the pine forest. The squirrels delayed their cutting of spruce cones, so that as yet that sure sign of early snows, the thud of dropping cones, did not disturb the peaceful solitude. The elk had not begun to bugle, the jays to squall, the wolves to mourn.

But passion, once awakened in Jake and Verde and at last realized, did not wait for the slow ripening of nature's fruitful season.

No Tonto youths ever let the autumn leaves heap round their long-spurred riding boots in the affairs of heart. They stormed the citadel and were seldom gentle about it. Jake and Verde had magnified in them all the elements of this primitive rock-bounded wilderness. They never rode to Tonto Flat together any more, but there was not one of the closing mellow days of October in which they did not ride to Kitty Mains' door. She found herself caught in her own devious toils. This fierce rivalry between two savage men was something new even to her experience. It frightened her.

For weeks the dances had been held at Tonto Flat and Green Valley, which were more accessible to the majority of Tonto Basin natives than the big log schoolhouse in the forest at the foot of the mountain slope. Here, in the years gone by, had taken place the important dances which had made history for the Tonto; and always the last dance of each season.

November came, with its still, blue-hazed mornings, and its warm, lazy, golden afternoons. But there seemed to be something exciting in the air, a cool breath in the silent forest. The deer had begun to range down from the heights.

Jake and Verde each had long solicited the honor of escorting Kitty Mains to this last dance of the season. In this instance they had given Kitty the privilege of choosing between them. She kept them waiting for her reply. Perhaps it was hard for her to make a decision—to show the Tonto people her preference. Perhaps she could not make up her mind which man she wanted to make happy and which she must hurt. Then perhaps she was afraid of this situation which she herself had brought about. In the end, and late in the day, she refused them both. It was probably the only instance, since her arrival at Tonto Flat, that she showed any strength of character.

On the day of this dance Jake came in from the woods to find Verde sitting aimlessly in the sun out by the log barn.

"Verde," he said, "Kitty sent me word late—she won't go with me tonight."

"Same here, Jake," replied Verde dejectedly.

"She's goin' with Ben Stillwell."

"No!"

"Sure, I heard so this mawnin'."

"Who told you?"

"I was down to the mesa an' dropped in

on the Browns. They had all the latest news. Tuck had just come home from town."

"How do you take this snub of Kitty's?"

"Me? I'm not takin' it at all," rejoined Jake darkly. "Reckon it's sort of a double-jointed slight. Kitty's too smart an' good to hurt one of us."

"I wonder," mused Verde.

"Reckon you savvy how she's upset you an' me?" asked Jake with eyes averted.

"Sure. But she cain't be blamed for that. We only got ourselves to blame."

"Hell of a mess!" mumbled Jake, and stood silent awhile, as if there was much to say, only he did not know what or how. These boys had not thought of each other for weeks. They were almost strangers now.

3

THE CHILL, MELANCHOLY TWILIGHT HAD SET-
tled down over the Tonto schoolhouse
when the first riders and wagons arrived.
The November wind moaned through the
pines. It bore an ominous note. A low
murmur of the swift creek rose from the
dark ravine. Voices, a girl's laugh, the
crack of iron-shod hoofs on stone echoed
through the forest.

Fires were built, one outside near the
great pile of wood cut for this occasion,
and another in the stove in one corner of
the large, empty, barnlike schoolroom.
The school benches had been arranged

25

around the walls. Half a dozen lamps emitted an uncertain, dim yellow flare.

Rapidly then the Tonto folk began to arrive, mostly on horseback, but many in wagons, buggies, buckboards. Soon a score or more of riotous children were making merry in the schoolroom. By seven o'clock there were over a hundred folk present, standing, talking, waiting, with more coming all the time.

Every time some newcomers entered the building there would be a stir and a buzz followed by hearty greetings. But when young Stillwell arrived, spick-and-span in his dark suit, and pale with suppressed excitement, leading a slender young woman wrapped in a fur coat, there was sudden cessation of sound.

They were not greeted until they reached the stove, and then a marked constraint seemed to attend the elders at least.

Kitty was cold, and said so in her sweet high treble. Stillwell removed her coat, to disclose her all in white, dainty and alluring, a girl for the backwoodsmen to feast their eyes upon, and over whom the women shook their heads silent and dubious.

But soon the old fiddler arrived with his fiddle, and the dance that would last till daylight was under way. The screaming children, darting among the dancers, were all that kept this annual festivity from being a strange, solemn affair. The young people took their dancing most seriously. There was no shyness, no immodesty, no ranting around, no loud talking, no forwardness; yet a blind man could have sensed that this was a courting business. Round and round the couples swayed in a moving circle, not ungraceful, not without rhythm, the young men with intent look and changeless faces; the girls rapt, absorbed; while the older folk looked on complacently and contentedly and the children played till from sheer exhaustion they fell asleep in the corner behind the stove, where blankets had been laid for them.

Jake and Verde rode down to the harvest dance together, though as uncommunicative as if miles of trail separated them. It was late when they reached the clearing and heard the fiddle and the steady shuffle of many feet. They unsaddled and blanketed their horses. As they approached the big outdoor fire to hold cold hands out to the blaze, the music ceased, and the shuffle of sliding feet changed, and there followed a merry roar of voices. Couples by the dozen emerged from the schoolhouse, some to pause by the fire, and others to wander off under the great solemn pines, close together, holding hands, whispering.

It was Jake who first confronted Kitty, to ask her for a dance. She was flushed, lovely, nervous, yet sincerely glad to see him.

"I've saved three, Jake," she replied, looking up to him with her strange eyes. "One for you and one for Verde—and another for you both to—"

"To fight over, huh?" he drawled. "Well, mebbe it won't come to that. An' Kitty, I'm takin' my dance out in talkin'.'"

"Oh, no, Jake. That'll spoil the whole evening for me," she pouted.

"Hope not. Anyway it goes."

In due time, when his dance came, Jake unceremoniously drew Kitty away from her admirers, and wrapping her in her coat, he led her out under the white cold stars, into the shadow of the pines. Here he took her little hands and drew her close.

"Kitty, this cain't go on any longer," he said.

"What?" she asked, trying to draw away.

"Why, this fast-an'-loose business. . . . You've kissed me, haven't you?"

"Well, no—not exactly," she demurred.

"Yes, you have. Anyway it was enough to let me kiss you—which is a fact as sure as Gawd looks down out of those stars on us. An' you swore you loved me."

"Of course I love you, Jake," she murmured, again her old capricious self, yet as if in earnest for once.

"That's tellin' me again, Kitty dear. That's the fast of it. But on the other hand you've denied it, flouted me, hurt me. That's the loose of it. . . . Wal, it cain't go on any longer."

"But, Jake, I can't help being myself," she replied rebelliously.

"Reckon I wouldn't have you no different," he went on. "But I love you somethin' turrible, an' if you play any more loose with me—there'll be—I—"

He choked and was silent. Then recovering, he went on in simple, intense eloquence to tell her of his love. She leaned against him, gazing up into his dark face, unresisting, carried away by the intensity of his love, reveling in it, finding in it all that she had yearned for, uplifted and transformed by the urgency and simplicity of his passion.

"An' now, Kitty, with it all told, I can

come to somethin' I've never said yet," he ended, his voice almost a whisper.

"Yes, Jake?" she whispered.

"Are you aimin' to spend the rest of your life here in the Tonto?"

"Why, of course. Father has got back his health. Mother likes the quiet—the green. And I—I love it."

"Then will you marry me?" he asked hoarsely.

"I will, Jake. I—I think I always meant to."

Later in the evening Verde presented himself for the dance that Kitty had promised him. Verde was so different from Jake. She trembled within. How handsome he was, and tonight how white his face and blazing his blue eyes!

"Kit, I reckon I don't care about dancin' this one little dance you've given me."

"Verde, you—you're not very complimentary. I'd love it," she replied, and it was the dancing devil eye that looked at him.

Verde did not ask her to go outdoors. He simply seized her arm and led the way. And when she demurred about going without her coat he said she would not need it.

"J-Jake and I had—a—an understanding," faltered Kitty.

"Reckon I'm powerful glad," he returned. "You an' I are goin' to have one too."

"Oh!" she exclaimed as he led her, with firm arm under hers, out under the very pine tree where only a short time before she had betrothed herself to Jake. Kitty divined at last that she had been made a victim of her own indiscretion. How could she tell Verde about Jake? Regret and an unfamiliar pang knocked at her heart. She had meant well. These backwoods brothers, this Damon and Pythias twain, had needed a lesson. But something had backfired. Verde was not like Jake, yet how wonderful he was!

"Ver—Verde, I'll freeze out here," she whispered, suddenly aware of the cold and of a chill that had nothing to do with the temperature.

For answer, Verde caught her up off the ground and like a great bear hugged her close to his breast. She could see his white face, radiant and beautiful in the starlight, yet somehow stern. She felt her breast swell against his.

"Kit, darlin', this is our understandin'," he whispered. "I reckon I've always been too easy with you. I never touched you—

like this—never kissed you before like I am—"

"Verde, you—you mustn't," she pleaded, trembling in his arms.

He kissed her lips. She cried out in protest, yet with the realization of a tide that she could not, did not, want to resist. But she gazed up at him, wide-eyed, fascinated, struggling to remember something. Her lips were parting to speak when he closed them with kisses, and then her eyes.

"Kit—I love—you so!" he said passionately, hoarsely, lifting his face from hers. "Say you love me . . . or I'll pack you on a hoss—off into the woods."

But Kitty could not speak.

"Say it!" he commanded, shaking her, and he kept it up until she slipped an arm around his neck.

Kitty was in a daze when once more she found herself among the dancers. Her partner, young Stillwell claimed her, but the dance had become a nightmare. All the gaiety and excitement of the occasion were gone.

The evening wore on toward the inevitable retribution which she knew was in store for her. At midnight a hearty supper was served. It was a hilarious occasion. Kitty's vague fears seemed lost, for the moment, and she was almost herself again. She dared not look at Jake or Verde, yet an almost irresistible longing to do so seized her as she sat on a school bench with young Stillwell.

At last the moment came when both Jack and Verde presented themselves for that third dance one of them was to get. Kitty seemed to sense that the hum of voices had ceased, to know that all the faces in the room were turned upon her, though a wave of terror was causing her to tremble as if from an ague.

"My dance, Kitty," drawled Jake.

"Well, Kit, I reckon this dance is mine," said Verde.

"I—I'll—divide it," she faltered, not looking up.

"Not with me, you won't," retorted Verde, his blue eyes flashing fire.

"Kitty, I hate to say it—but I cain't share this with Verde," said Jake.

"But I didn't promise it to either of you," she barely whispered.

"Not in so many words," returned Jake, attempting to grab her hand.

That was the torch. Verde turned to Jake.

"Are you disputin' my lady friend's word?" he asked belligerently.

"Sure am," replied Jake coolly.

Verde stepped forward and slapped his brother's face, not violently, but with what seemed to be slow deliberation.

With the suddenness of a panther Jake lunged out to knock Verde down. Kitty screamed. The crowd gasped, then fell silent. Slowly Verde raised himself on his elbow. His face was changing quickly from red to white. He stretched up his free arm, and his extended fingers quivered.

"Jake!"

"Get up an' ask the lady's pardon," demanded Jake wildly.

"You hit me!" exclaimed Verde unbelievingly.

"Nope. I just blowed a thistledown at you," replied Jake.

In one single bound Verde was on his feet. Tearing off coat and tie, he confronted the man who had been almost a brother to him. "Come out!" he challenged, his voice hoarse with rage. The circle of startled onlookers parted.

In another moment they stood face to face in the light of the roaring bonfire. The crowd of men and boys, and a few of the girls, had poured out after them.

Then like two mad bulls Jake and Verde rushed at each other. They gave flailing blow for flailing blow. They danced around in the red firelight, seeking an opening to deliver damaging blows that were intended to hurt and to maim. Tonto fights were usually marked by hilarity among the spectators. But there was none here. This was strange, unnatural, hateful—to watch these friends and brothers so deadly, so cold and savage, with murder in their every action.

Their white faces and white shirts soon were bloody. They fought for a long time, erect and silent, knocking each other down, leaping up and rushing in again. Then they clinched, and wrestling, stumbling, they fell to roll over and over on the ground.

That battle between the Duntons was the worst that had ever been fought at the old schoolhouse. It lasted two hours, and ended with Jake lying unconscious and bedraggled in the mud, and Verde, hideously marked and bloody, staggering to his feet and out into the gloom of the forest.

4

Jake had been so badly beaten that he was in bed for a week, during which time he saw only his mother. In summer and fall he and Verde always slept in the loft over the porch. But Verde had not been there now for many days.

During this week of pain and shame, Jake's mind had been a numbed thing, dark and set and sinister. He could not think beyond the fact that he had been terribly whipped and disgraced before a crowd of Tonto folk, one of whom had been Kitty Mains. She had seen him stretched in the mud, at the hands of Verde. His battered face burned with the disgrace of it. His scarred fists clenched and unclenched impatiently.

Jake always turned his bruised and beaten face to the wall when his mother climbed the ladder to the loft, bringing food and drink he did not want and which he had to force himself to take. She had ceased her importunities on behalf of Verde. They were useless.

At last Jake crawled down out of his hole, feeling as mean as he knew he looked. He wanted to get away into the woods quickly before anyone saw him! That was the only thought in his mind.

But while he was packing his outfit his father suddenly confronted him.

"Your ma said there ain't no use of talkin' to you," he began gruffly.

"Reckon not," replied Jake, turning away the face he was ashamed to reveal.

"Wal, I'll have a word anyhow," rejoined the father. "From now on is this heah Tonto Basin goin' to be big enough for you an' Verde?"

"Hell no!"

"Ahuh, I reckoned so, an' it's shore a pity," said Dunton sadly.

"Where is Verde?" asked Jake.

"I don't know. He never come home. But he sent word that if you wanted satisfaction you'd know where to find him."

Jake made no reply. A smoldering fire of hatred within him would not let him speak to those who loved him. Old Dunton hung around, lending a hand at his son's packing.

"Wal, I see you're off to set a string of traps," he finally forced himself to say. "It's a plumb good idea. Work's most all done for the fall, an' I can spare you. Mebbe you'll be better for a lonesome trip. Nothin' like the woods to cure a feller of most anythin'. But, Jake, I don't like the look an' feel of the weather. If I don't disremember, it was this way one fall fifteen years ago. No rain. Late frost. Winter holdin' off. But, Lord—when she broke! . . . Washed the cabin away, that storm!"

"It's all one to me, Pa," replied Jake dully. And leading his pack horse, Jake rode away from the ranch without thinking to bid his parents good-by.

The day fitted Jake's mood. The sky was overcast, dull, leaden gray, gloomy and forbidding, with a dim sun showing red in the west. The fall wind mourned through the pines. It was cold and raw, whipping up into gusts at times, then subsiding again. The creek had run so low that now it scarcely made any sound on its way down to the valley. Jake rode out of the pines down into the cedars and oaks and sycamores. In the still pools of water the bronze and yellow leaves floated round and round.

At length Jake reached the junction of the trail with the highway, and soon came to where it crossed the Verde Creek. Lost Boy Ford! He had never forgotten, until these last bitter weeks, the significance of this place. For a few moments a terrific strife warred within him. But he quelled it. Nothing could stand against his jealousy and his shame. Kitty loved him dearest and best, but she must also have loved Verde, or he never would have acted as he had. The Tonto Valley was not large enough for both Verde and him. Who would have to go? That would have to be decided; and as Jake knew that neither he nor Verde would ever relinquish the field to the other, it seemed settled that death must step in for the decision. Jake realized now that he was no match for Verde in the rough and terrible Tonto method of fighting; on the other hand, he knew that in a battle with weapons such as must decide this bitter feud he would kill Verde. And such was the dark and fierce violence to which his passion had mounted that he brooded with savage an-

ticipation over his power to rid himself
forever of his rival.

Soon he headed off the road into the
thickets of scrub oak and jack pine, manzanita and mescal, and began to climb an
old unused trail. It led up over the slope
to the mesa, into the cedars and piñons
and junipers, and at last into the somber
forest again.

Here it was like twilight, cool, still, and
lonely. The peace of the wilderness tried
to pierce Jake's brooding, bitter thoughts,
and for the first time in his life it failed.
A monstrous wall of bitterness seemed to
enclose him.

He climbed high, riding for miles, in a
multitude of detours and zigzags, along a
trail thousands of feet above the basin below. The slopes grew exceedingly steep
and rough. In many places he dismounted
to make his way on foot. How dry the
brush and soil! The tufts of grass were
sere and brown; the dead manzanita
broke off like icicles.

At length he arrived at the base of the
rim wall. It towered above, seemingly to
the sky. A trail ran along the irregular
stone cliff, and there were fresh hoof
tracks on it. They had been made by
Verde's horse, and were a day or two old,
perhaps a little more. If Jake had felt any

uncertainty it ended right there. Verde had indeed known where to come to give him satisfaction.

Jake rode on to a corner of the wall. Here the trail plunged down. A mighty amphitheater opened in the rim. It was miles across and extended far back. All around it capes and escarpments loomed out over the colorful abyss.

It seemed to be a scene of dying fires. The ragged gold of the aspens showed dim against the scarlet maples, the red sumac, the bronze oaks, the magenta gums, and all the dark greens. Yellow crags leaned with their great slabs of rock over the void. Here and there gleamed cliffs of dull pink, with black eyelike caves. Far down in the middle of this gulf there was a dark canyon. Black Gorge!

This was Jake's objective. He gazed down with narrowed eyes, strangely magnifying. Ten years before he and Verde had discovered by accident a way to get down into this almost inaccessible fastness under the rim. They had named it Black Gorge. No other trappers or hunters or riders had ever penetrated it. As boys they had made it their rendezvous, Jake to trap and hunt, Verde to corral his wild horses. They went there several times each year, usually together, but sometimes alone. It grew to mean much to them, and they loved it.

"Verde is down there waitin'," muttered Jake, and the somber shadow that had closed over his mind seemed to come between his eyes and the wonderful beauty of the scene.

A sudden rush of wind, wailing in the niches of the cliff overhead, turned Jake's thoughts to the weather. The habit of observation was strong in him. He gazed down and across the basin. And he was suddenly amazed by the sight he saw.

He had seen all kinds of light and cloud effects over the vast valley before, but never before one of such weird, sinister aspect. The sun was westering over the Mazatzals, and through the dark riven pall of cloud it shed a gleam of angry red. From the southwest a lowering multitude of pale little clouds came scudding toward the rim. They were the heralds of storm. But as yet, except for the moan of the wind along the cliff, there was no sound. The basin lay deep in shadow. The cold gray tones near at hand, the smoky sulphurous red of the sunset, the utter solitude of the scene, the vast saw-toothed gap in the rim wall, the distant forbidding shadow of Black Gorge, the bleak November day that was to mark the end of the lingering autumn, the all-pervading spirit of nature's inevitable and ruthless change from lull to storm, from peace to strife, from the saving and fruitful weeks of the past to the ominous promise of sudden storm and destruction—all these permeated Jake's being, and possessed him utterly, and sent him down the trail deaf at last to a still small voice that had been whispering faintly, yet persistently at the closed door of his heart.

5

THERE WAS ONLY ONE ENTRANCE TO BLACK
Gorge that Jake had ever been able to dis-
cover. He had found various slopes along
its three-mile zigzag length where an Indian or an agile young man might by supreme pluck and exertion climb out. But
for the most part it was as unscalable as
it was inaccessible. A signal proof of the
nature of Black Gorge was the fact that
in the late fall only a few deer and no bear
frequented it.

While it required hours to climb out by
the only trail Jake knew, it took but a
short time to make the descent. Without
a horse Jake could get down in less than

a quarter of an hour. That, however, was practically by sliding down. Now, with saddle and pack horse, Jake had all he could do to keep the three of them together. Finally his saddle horse got ahead. Several times the pack animal slipped; and it was difficult to adjust the ropes and bags on the almost perpendicular slope.

Black Gorge deserved its name. It would have been black even without the somber, fading twilight. The walls of stone were stained dark, and in places where ledges and steps and slopes broke the sheer, perpendicular line, brush and moss and vines mantled them so thickly that they looked black in the gloom. At the lower end of the gorge, where Jake had descended, the stream had no outlet. The creek was dry now, but when water flowed there it merely sank into the jumble of mighty mossy boulders. Once no doubt there had been an outlet, but it had been choked by the fall of a splintered cliff.

Jake mounted to ride up a narrow defile. He was concerned at the moment about the water. Black Gorge had never, to his knowledge, been completely dry. But far up the gorge he knew of a spring that ought still to be alive. Besides, he began to feel a cool misty rain on his face.

At this moment his mind reverted again to Verde. In the gathering gloom he could not see the trail, but he had no doubt about Verde's tracks being there. He almost reined in his horse so he could wait and think what to do. But there was nothing more to be considered on that score. It was settled. When he faced Verde again, there would be need of but a few words. The rest would be action. Even so, Jake felt a monstrous hand at the back of him, propelling him toward something that he had gladly and sternly willed, yet against which at odd moments his soul revolted.

The gorge widened, the walls ceased to tower and lean, the slopes slanted up out of sight, and the gray gloom lightened considerably. The trail climbed from the dry stream bed to a bench that soon grew level. Jake heard the clucking of wild turkeys and then the booming flap of heavy wings in the branches of a tree. Toward the upper end this bench held a fine open grove of pines and spruce. Jake saw the dark spear-pointed spruce that towered above the little log cabin he and Verde had built there years ago. So long ago and far away those years seemed now!

Jake's instinct was to dismount and draw a gun. Not to be ambushed or surprised! But he cursed the thought that was so unfamiliar to him.

His expectation was to see the light of a campfire, or a flickering gleam from the door of the cabin, as he had many and many a time beheld with glad eyes. But the familiar space was blank, the cabin dark. Jake dismounted, and throwing his bridle, with slow step went forward. The cabin was deserted. It smelled dry and musty. No fire had been kindled there for a long time. He heard the rustling of mice and felt the wind of bats flying close by his head.

Verde might have come, but he was not there now. Sudden, strange relief swept over Jake. He sank to a seat on the step on the edge of the little porch. His sombrero fell off unheeded, and the cold misty rain touched his face. His heart labored as though after a long strain. He sat there in the lonely, silent gorge, vaguely, dully conscious of an agony deep hidden somewhere under the weight of other emotions. It passed, and he addressed himself to the necessary task.

He unsaddled and unpacked, and turned the horses loose, with the thought that it was well for them a storm was brewing. Then he carried his packs and saddle inside the cabin, and set about building a fire in the rude stone fireplace. He appeared slow and awkward. Not only were his fingers all thumbs, but they also trembled in a way quite incomprehensible to him.

"Reckon I'm cold and hungry," he thought.

Every few moments, while cooking supper, which he quite unconsciously planned for two, he would halt in his preparations and listen for the thud of hoofs or the jangle of spurs. But he heard only the melancholy wail of the rising wind.

Presently he stuck a dry fagot of pitch pine into the fire, and with a blazing torch he went outside the cabin to search in the dust for tracks. He found only his own and those made by his horses. Not satisfied, he made a more thorough search. But it was all in vain!

"Verde hasn't been here," he muttered at last, and pondered the situation. There was absolutely no doubt about the fact of Verde's fresh tracks in the trail above the gorge. What had delayed him? And Jake reminded himself of Verde's impetuosity and recklessness on bad trails.

Jake went back into the cabin, where, as many times before, he set some food and drink to keep hot in case Verde might arrive late. Then he unrolled his bed on the heavy mat of dry spruce boughs. This done, he stepped out again. The darkness was like pitch. High up there along the black rim the wind made a low, dismal roaring sound. He could see the leaden band of sky between the two black rims.

He returned presently to the warm fireside, to which he extended his nervous hands. He faced the fire awhile. That had always been one of his joys. But tonight it was not a joy. An arch face suddenly shone out of the glow—a girl's face, roguish, sweet red lips and strange, unmatched, inviting eyes. Jake had to turn his back to them.

It struck him singularly that Kitty Mains' face in the embers of this cabin fire was something he had never before beheld there. She was something new. She did not belong to that cabin. Thought of her seemed out of place there. He did not even want to think of her now.

When the fire died low Jake went to bed. He was tired and his eyes were heavy. Sleep at last overcame his mind.

In the night he awoke. A tiny pattering of rain sounded on the roof. The wind had lulled somewhat. The night was so black he could not see the door or window. He could tell that the hour was late, for he had rested. And gradually he grew wide awake. The pattering rain ceased, came again in little gusts, died away, only to return. It recalled to Jake that his father had once forbidden him and Verde to camp very late in the fall at this Black Gorge cabin. A blizzard such as sometimes set in after a late fall might snow them in for the whole winter. Jake had completely forgotten this. Likewise had Verde, or if he had not forgotten, he had come anyway. Black Gorge was the one hiding place where they would not be disturbed. His father knew of it, yet could never have found the way there.

The rain pattered again, slightly harder, and a wind sighed in the pines and spruces over the cabin. Suddenly a low, distant, rumble startled Jake. Thunder! He sat up in bed, listening. A thunderclap late in the fall was rare and always preceded a terrible storm. Possibly he was mistaken. Sometimes rocks rolled down in distant canyons, making a sound like thunder.

Slowly Jake settled back in his blankets, his alarm dispelled. The rain grew into a steady low roar. Then it fell away for a while. The night wind lulled again.

Silence and blackness lay like weights upon Jake's senses.

Then the ebony darkness split. An appalling white light flashed through the open door. The cabin was illuminated with the brightness of noonday. Outside, the black pines stood up against the blue-white glare, the black jaws of the gorge seemed to be snapping at the angry sky. Then thunder crashed with a deafening blast. The cabin shook. The sharp explosion changed to boom and bellow, filling the narrow gorge with reverberating echoes, endlessly repeated until they rumbled away into utter silence.

Uncertainty ceased for Jake Dunton. The long, late Indian summer, so colorful and mellow and fruitful, must be paid for in the harsh terms with which nature always audited her account in the Tonto. Jake forgot his mission there in the realization that fate had shut him in Black Gorge on the eve of a blizzard. At the moment the peril did not strike him. He reacted as he might have on any of the other numerous sojourns in this canyon. He thought of Verde out there somewhere in the blackness.

"Damn Verde anyhow," complained Jake. "Why won't he ever listen to me?"

The pattering rain commenced again,

and this time did not cease. Nor did the wind lull. Both perceptibly augmented, but so slowly as to persuade the lonely listener against his better judgment. They bade him hope against hope.

Then the storm broke with savage and demoniac fury. There was no more thunder, or at least in the mighty roar of wind and water Jake could not distinguish any. It took all Jake's strength to close the cabin door. He went back to bed, thankful for the impervious roof he and Verde had built on the cabin, and for the safe site they had chosen.

His ears became filled with an infernal din. The gorge might have become the battleground of all the elements from the beginning of time. Jake had never experienced such screaming of winds, such a torrential deluge of rain. He lay there, forgetting himself, fearful only for the lost Verde. Verde, the boy—lost again! And each terrible hour the storm gained in strength, changing, swelling, mounting to cataclysmic force.

Toward dawn, which he ascertained by a grayness superseding the pitch blackness, there came a gradual lessening of the deluge and lulls in the bellowing of the wind.

Day broke leaden, gusty, with signs of

the inevitable change from rain to snow. Jake struck a fire and then went out to look around.

Well indeed was it that the cabin had been erected on a bench high above the stream bed. Where last night had been a rough boulder and gravel-strewn gully, there was now a lake. What amazed Jake was the fact that he could not note any current. Perhaps it was because of the enormous volume of water that must be draining out of the gorge; and the underground exit was not large enough to take care of it. Nevertheless, that theory did not wholly satisfy Jake.

Thin yellow sheets of water were falling from the cliffs, and here and there narrow torrents rushed pell-mell down the cracks and defiles of the slopes.

Jake gazed up at the dark, leaden sky. The storm clouds had lodged against the rim and hung there. Only in a few places could he see the ramparts, with the gray wall fringed by black pine. The air was still warm, but a gust of wind now and then brought a cold raw breath. During the day, or more likely when night fell, the rain would turn to snow.

6

Jake WENT INTO THE CABIN TO COOK BREAK-
fast. The situation was beyond him. By all
the woodcraft of which he was master, he
knew that the imperative need was to
climb out of the gorge before the snow
made it impossible. If it had not been for
the certainty of Verde's horse tracks on
the trail Jake would have attempted to escape at once. But he well knew that Verde
would not leave, even if he were able. Jake
had no alternative. How futile now that a
few hours of oblivion in sleep had brought
his mind back toward normal! The die
was cast. The catastrophe of a great
storm could not make the situation any

more desperate for him and Verde. But it made him think; and he had to deny the reason that began to dispel his passion of the past few weeks.

Methodically Jake went about his preparations for breakfast. He was a good cook and had always taken pride in the accomplishment. His keen sensibilities, however, were wholly absorbed in things outside the cabin—the moan of the wind rising again, the frequent rain squalls, the increasing roar of falling water. With some feeling that he could not understand he did not expect Verde, yet he listened for the sound of hoofs or the jangle of spurs.

He poured a second cup of coffee. Lifting the cup, he was about to drink when something happened wholly new in his experience. He wanted to drink, but could not.

Halfway to his lips the full cup poised.

Jake stared. The coffee was quivering.

"Gosh! Am I that nervous?" he exclaimed, and he set the cup down on a bench.

But the coffee continued to quiver. Indeed, the motion increased. There were queer little circles and waves inside the cup!

"Reckon I'm loco," muttered Jake. Nevertheless, he strained his faculties. Something was wrong. In him, for a certainty, but also outside! He continued to stare at the coffee in the cup. Then he heard the rustling of the dry spruce boughs under his bed. Mice! He thought it rather an odd hour for mice to begin emerging. Next a faint rattling of the loft poles attracted his attention.

The whole cabin was shaking. Jake leaped to his feet, and rushed toward the door. The tremor increased. His cooking utensils began to clatter. The cans on the shelves took to dancing. The earth under the cabin was trembling.

A rumbling sound filled Jake's ears. Thunder! The storm was about to break into its second and most fearful phase. It was a long, low, dull roar, gaining volume at the end instead of dying away! Was that thunder?

"Avalanche!" yelled Jake, and bounded wildly out of the cabin.

In the open he halted. His terror had been absurd. The cabin was so situated that no earth slide or rolling rocks could reach it.

Then his gaze fixed upon the stretch of gorge below. He could see to the narrow passage between the black walls through which he had come last night. Everywhere water was running off the cliffs. The canyon appeared to be wreathed in waterfalls, lacy, thin, yellow, with some like ragged ribbons of water.

The sound that had alarmed Jake did not cease. It grew in intensity. Slides of weathered rock on the slopes above! His keen eye sought the heights.

The skyline of the rim wall had changed. Could it be hidden in cloud? But the gray pall hung above and beyond. There seemed to be movement, either of a drifting veil of rain or a long section of slope. Jake wondered if his eyes were deceiving him. Had his love for Verde and Kitty, the jealousy and the fight and the hate, and the dreadful night of storm unhinged his mind? Was he going crazy?

No! His eagle eye had the truth at last. A section of the rim wall had slipped and was sliding down toward the lower end of Black Gorge.

Jake stood there, motionless and dumb with mingled terror and awe. The section of the rim, with its fringe of black pines erect, was moving downward with a gathering and ponderous momentum. The rumble increased to thunder.

A cloud of yellow dust began to lift against the background of stone wall and leaden sky, quickly blotting them out.

Jake's straining sight recorded what seemed to be an illusion in his stunned mind. The line of erect pine trees turned at right angles, and the black spear-tipped trees pointed out over the gorge. Then they waved and dipped. The line broke, the trees leaned and whirled and fell, to be swallowed up by the sliding slope. Only the thundering, rending roar gave reality to what Jake saw. The section of rim wall, giving way, had started the whole slope below into a colossal avalanche. It was a brain-numbing spectacle! The vast green slope of cedar and piñon, of manzanita and oak, of yellow crag and red earth, had become a swelling, undulating cataract. It was beautiful, awe-inspiring. Only the cataclysmic sound rendered proof of its destructive force.

But in a few more seconds the grace and rhythmic movement gave place to upheaval, and then to a tremendous volleying of boulders flung ahead of the avalanche. Rocks as large as cabins hurdled the narrow split of Black Gorge. Large and small they began to crack like cannon balls against the far wall of the gorge.

Jake could see, at the instant when the green mass reached the verge, the width of canyon light streaked by multitudes of falling rocks. Then the avalanche, like a vast, tumbling waterfall of rocks and debris, slid over to fill the end of the gorge.

A terrific wind, propelled up the canyon, staggered Jake. The roar that had grown awful ceased to be sound. He heard no more.

The lower end of Black Gorge was buried by an avalanche that concealed its crushed and splintered mass of debris under a mantle of dust. The lake that had formed at the lower end of the gorge, and which had been displaced by the avalanche now, came swelling and rushing back like a flooded river breaking through its dikes, and the waters rose halfway up to where the cabin stood on the wide bench.

Jake's first realization of a recovered sense of hearing came with this sound of the chafing flood waters. The contrast between the roar that had deafened him and the gentle lapping of the waves left his ears ringing.

The avalanche had come to rest under its sky-high dust cloud.

Jake ran down the trail and off the bench as far as he could go. Through the thinning dust curtain he saw the width of the gorge piled almost straight up with fresh red earth, skinned tree trunks, and rocks of every size. The avalanche had filled the gorge beyond the narrow defile. Its destructive force had extended to a point even beyond the limit of its wall. Jake had to find a new path between boulders higher than his head, and over logs and slides of shale.

Rocks were still rolling down under the veil of dust. And Jake thought it would be well to retreat to the cabin. Just as he turned back he heard a cry that froze his blood.

Breathless, with heart pounding in his breast, he listened. More than once in his life had he heard the shrill sound made by a horse in extreme terror or injured near to death. This was how Jake interpreted the sound. His heart jumped and he began to breathe again. Then the cry pealed out louder than before.

Jake began frantically climbing in the direction from which he thought the horse's scream had come. The going was rough, over the loose debris flung off by the avalanche. He reached the line of trees and more level ground. It was wet and very slippery. Rain mixed with snow fell around him.

Then suddenly, close at hand, there rose a harsh, fierce shout. It seemed to Jake that he recognized Verde's voice. He bounded through the wet brush and under the dripping trees.

A moment later he burst into a little glade, across which a good-sized pine had fallen. And on the side toward Jake, close to the wet earth, protruded a pair of boots equipped with long bright spurs. Jake recognized them. They did not move. The legs which wore them were pinned to the ground!

Like a panther, Jake leaped over the log. He found himself looking down into the ash-white, agonized face of Verde. The youth still was conscious. His eyes moved and fixed in an expression of disbelief on Jake's face. Then recognition came and he murmured, "Jake."

"My Gawd—Verde!" cried Jake, falling upon his knees to grasp Verde's writhing hands.

"It got me—Jake," whispered Verde. "Last night—my horse fell on me—broke my leg. . . . I crawled—this far—then—the avalanche—"

"I'll get you out, Verde," declared Jake, and laying hold of the prostrate form, he started to pull.

Verde cursed and beat at his rescuer until he ceased his efforts to drag the fallen man from under the tree trunk.

"Don't," whispered Verde, his face

white and drawn, wet with big clammy drops of sweat, and jaw quivering. "Don't touch me. . . . I'm done for. . . . But thank Gawd—you've come to—end my misery."

Then Jake awoke to the horror of the facts. Verde lay crushed beneath the pine. It had caught him across the legs almost to the hips. Jake saw a white leg bone protruding through Verde's overalls. The end of the bone was black with dirt.

If there were other bodily injuries, as no doubt there were, Jake could not see them. Verde's arms were free, his chest was apparently sound. But there was a bloody cut on his head.

Again Verde screamed and the unearthly sound broke Jake's nerve and strength. He let go, shaking in every nerve of his body. He had seen another leg bone come protruding out, bloody and white, through Verde's overalls.

"For Gawd's sake, man," panted Verde, "don't let me die by slow torture this way!"

He lay there, transfixing Jake with eyes Jake found almost unendurable to meet.

"Jake—old boy—fer the love of Gawd, put me out—of my misery!"

Jake could only shake his head slowly.

"Shoot me, Jake. . . . I cain't stand it. . . .

No use anyhow. . . . I'm smashed. . . . Kill me!"

"Verde!"

"Don't waste time!" pleaded Verde, the blue fire of his eyes momentarily burning away the mist of anguish. "Every second is worse than hellfire! . . . If you have any mercy—kill me!"

"No!"

"But Jake—dear old brother—you don't savvy," went on the pleading husky voice. "I'll bless you—in the hereafter. . . . I beg you. . . . Jake, you saved me once—when we were—young 'uns. You know—down at Lost Boy Ford! You were brother to me then—an' always you've been. . . . But now the great thing is—to spare me— more of this. . . . Cain't you see? Why, old boy, I'd do it—fer you. . . . I swear to Gawd I would. . . . Jake—if you—love me—end my misery!"

Jake's nerveless hand groped for his gun. He seemed numbed. All the sweetness of the years rushed into this one supreme moment—unbearable in its heart-shocking agony.

Verde was praying now for deliverance. The deathly radiance of his face seemed to come already from that other world he sought. His face was almost unearthly beautiful then—and it seemed as if the power to command came from beyond life itself. For a moment he almost overcame Jake's resistance. But now a strength almost as great as the avalanche that had caught them seized upon Jake's heart and mind, and the spell was broken.

When Verde saw that he had failed, he snatched at Jake's gun with a wild and tortured cry. Jake flung it far from him.

Then Verde sank back unconscious. And Jake, whipping out his knife, began to dig frantically at the soft earth under Verde's imprisoned legs.

He scooped out a hole on one side, then on the other. Presently he reached under the tree and dug farther. In a few more moments he was able to drag Verde gently from under the log that had imprisoned him.

Then he knelt beside the still form, not daring to look at the white face. He placed a shaking, muddy hand on Verde's breast. Verde's heart still was beating faintly. Realization that his brother still lived made a giant out of Jake.

Sheathing the knife, he lifted the limp form in his arms and strode down to the trail.

The rain had let up a little. The dust was settling. And there came a brightening of the sky, one of the false hopes that such storms hold out in their early stages. As he reached the cabin he noted that the rain was changing to snow.

7

VERDE OPENED HIS EYES. HE SMELLED SMOKE and heard the crackling of a fire. A roof of rough-hewn poles and split shingles slanted above him. He recognized the cabin, and then in a flash he recalled the chain of circumstances that had led to his presence there.

He lay on a couch of boughs in the corner of the cabin. A blanket covered him. Jake was not in the room. Verde felt that the lower parts of his limbs were dead. He had a locked, icy sensation in his breast. He found that he had free use of his hands, and could move his head without difficulty. Jake had removed his boots, one of which had been slit. A bloody ragged leg of his trousers hung over a bench.

The door of the cabin stood open. Verde saw whirling, thin-flaked snow. The ground bore a mantle of white, and the spruce trees looked spectral against the gray gloom. A sound of falling water filled the cabin.

Rapid footfalls struck his ear. The doorway darkened. Jake entered staggering under an enormous armload of fagots. He was wet, and brought in the dank odor of pine. Not until he had deposited the load of wood in a corner next to the huge stone fireplace did he observe that Verde was conscious.

"By glory—you've come to!" he exclaimed, and the haggard darkness of his face brightened in a homely grin.

"Reckon—I have," replied Verde. Speaking was difficult and his voice pitifully weak.

"It took so long," said Jake, with immense relief. "I thought—I was afraid. . . . Verde, are you sufferin'—much?"

"Cain't tell. Feel daid in my legs an' sort of queer here," rejoined Verde, indicating his breast.

"I'm thankful you've no orful pain like this mawnin'."

"What time of day is it?"

"Late afternoon."

"An' I've been unconscious all day long?"

"You shore have."

They looked long into each other's face. Verde's faculties were growing acute. He saw that Jake was laboring under an enormous strain. How strange! Jake was usually so cool, so easy, so sure.

"Jake, old boy, how bad am I hurt?"

"Turrible—bad—all right," replied Jake, swallowing hard.

"Wal, just how and where?"

"There's a cut on your head, clear to the bone. Your right leg is broke below the knee. One bone. I set thet—an' got it in splints. But your—left leg—"

"Got you stumped, hey?" asked Verde as Jake shook his head and gulped.

"Smashed—an' the bones splintered all to hell."

"Ahuh! Must have bled a lot."

"Bled? You shore bled like a stuck pig. But I got thet stopped."

"Wal, is that all, Jake? Honest Injun now?"

"All I'm sure about. First off there was blood runnin' from your mouth. That scared me. But you haven't bled any more fer hours."

"Ahuh! ... An' what else are we up against, old boy?"

Jake lifted his hands in a helpless, half-frantic gesture of despair.

"Verde! If the avalanche didn't shut us in forever we're shore snowed up for the winter."

"I was figurin' somethin' like," replied Verde quietly, and closed his eyes. He could not endure to look at Jake any longer just then. Jake was more than appalled by the tragedy. And Verde began to ponder over a meaning for it.

"Verde, you asked me to be honest," went on Jake hesitantly. "An I'm tellin' you—only a miracle can save us."

Verde noted that Jake used the plural. Perhaps it was only a slip of speech in the seriousness of the moment. Still the implication of a prayer for that one saving miracle was strong. From under his half-closed eyelids Verde watched Jake as he busied himself over the cooking utensils and the fire. Anyone who knew Jake could have told that he was not himself. He was restless, exceedingly nervous, now hurried and again abstracted. He would seem to forget the meal he was preparing and then he would suddenly remember it. He walked aimlessly about the room, took up tasks irrelevant to the hour and left them abruptly, unfinished. He went outdoors and returned for no reason that was evident. Once he came in with an armload of wood, only to carry it out again. And always the only consistent action he seemed to be performing was to turn every little while tragic, deep-set, fearful eyes in the direction of Verde.

At last he managed to get supper ready. "Verde, can you eat or drink?" he asked.

"I crave cold water. Thet's all. Put some snow in it," replied Verde.

Jake brought it and set it at Verde's elbow.

The afternoon waned and soon night fell. The soft, seeping, sweeping, rustling sound of falling snow almost imperceptibly increased. Around the eaves of the cabin and in the spruces the wind sighed mournfully. From the heights came the faint roar of the storm.

Jake sat in the firelight and Verde watched him. It must have continued so for a long time. Often Jake would replenish the dying fire, which would crackle and flare up and again light up the cabin. It seemed to Verde that Jake was trying not to surrender to a situation that he knew was hopeless. First the natural shock following the desperate accident to

Verde, and now the realization of their being shut in, surely lost together. Verde read it all in Jake's dark face.

Jake had meant to kill him. He had wanted him dead! In the humiliation of being whipped before their friends and relatives, and in the jealousy of the hour, and in the subsequent recognition that Kitty Mains loved him no more than she loved Verde, Jake had succumbed to the lust to kill.

When Verde sent word to Jake that he knew where to find him if he wanted satisfaction, Verde had hoped nothing more would come of it. Nothing more except that Kitty should choose one of them! He had hoped, but he had doubted. And here they were, doomed by the avalanche to the same fate. And poor Jake had awakened too late from the horror of his hate for him. It was Jake's fault that they had come to Black Gorge at a season when they should have shunned it. His fault, too, the horror of Verde's crushed legs and the lingering death to come!

In the dark lonely hours of that night, when the flickering firelight played upon Jake's tortured face, Verde learned how awful it must be for Jake. For himself he did not care. Even if he could have been saved he would not have welcomed it. What good of life hobbling about on maimed legs? But for Jake's sake he began to want to live. And as the hours dragged by this desire grew.

Toward morning Jake tiptoed over to peer down at Verde, and then, thinking him asleep, he lay down beside him, very quietly.

But Verde was far from asleep. The pangs of agony had reawakened in his numbed leg. The fire flickered, casting its fantastic shadows on the rude walls of the cabin, flickered, faded, and died. Then blackness reigned. Outside the snow seeped and whirled and, with silky rustle, beat against the cabin. Sometimes vagrant flakes blew through the little window and fell cool and wet upon Verde's face. The wind mourned. Once when it lulled Verde heard the wild, lonely cry of a wolf.

Verde's body seemed weighted by lead. The desperate desire to move had to be yielded to. And the slightest movement of his lower muscles was equivalent to plunging ten thousand red-hot spikes into his quivering flesh. But he endured, and fought the strange indifference that stole over his mind.

He must live for Jake's sake. Jake—who

had wanted him dead! What a queer thing—that Jake could have imagined that he would be happier with his old friend out of the way!

Dawn broke. Verde was careful to look wide-awake and more cheerful when Jake turned to him.

"How are you, Verde?"

"Rarin' to go—if we only could," replied Verde. "Pile out, Jake, an' when you've had breakfast I want to talk to you."

"Verde! You're not sinkin'?"

"Would you expect me to be soarin'? I haven't sprouted wings yet," returned Verde.

Jake moved about with a synthetic haste that would have been ludicrous if it had not been so pathetic. Every one of his actions proved that he believed his earnestness futile.

"Open the door an' let's look out," said Verde.

Black Gorge was now white, except for the lake which had risen nearly to the edge of the bench.

"Reckon it won't snow heavy down heah," rejoined Jake.

"Is the air cold? I don't 'pear to feel it."

"Nope. It's warm yet, an' that means more snow. But winter shore has set in."

"Wal, Jake, let's talk," replied Verde. "Leave the door open so it'll be light."

Jake drew a bench to Verde's bedside and looked down upon him with the miserable eyes of a dog that knows it has been beaten.

"All right, Verde, I'll listen," he said. But there was not the slightest indication of hope in look or tone.

"What's to be done?" asked Verde brightly.

Jake spread wide his hands with an air of dejection.

"Jake, you've got it figgered this way," went on Verde. "Nobody could get to us, even if they knew where we are. We cain't climb out in the snow. An' I've got to die pronto—an' then you'll starve to death?"

"Not starve, Verde," returned Jake hoarsely. But he had acquiesced with Verde's summary of the situation. He dropped his face in his big broad hands, and tears trickled between his fingers.

"Miracles do happen, Jake," said Verde.

Jake made a sharp gesture of despair.

"Yes. Dad might find us. But even so—he couldn't save you."

"Old boy, is that what matters so much?" asked Verde softly.

"Reckon it's all—that—matters," replied Jake brokenly.

"Well, then, you must be up an' doin'."

"Verde, my mind's stopped workin'."

"Mine hasn't, an' don't you forget it," returned Verde. "Mine's just begun. . . . Jake, you know that my leg as it is—all smashed—will soon mortify. An' it'd kill me pronto."

"Hell, man! You needn't tell me that," Jake replied.

"You've got to cut my leg off," returned Verde slowly and evenly.

"My Gawd, Verde! . . . I—I couldn't," gasped Jake.

"Sure you could. Now think sense, Jake. It's my only chance. You could cut it off—if I told you how—an' if I'd stand it."

Jake was pale and sweating. His big hands opened and shut. His homely, battered face was working.

"Yes, I might. It's this idea that takes my nerve. . . . You—you might die while I was doin' it!"

"Of course I might. That's the chance. But I think I wouldn't. An' it's damn sure I'll die if you don't. Let's take the chance—my only chance."

"Lord, if I had the nerve!" cried Jake, and he leaped up to pace the room.

"Come back here. . . . Now listen," went on Verde, growing inspired with his plan. "I tell you it's a great idea. An' you can do it!"

"How about the big arteries in your leg?" Jake boomed. "I had one hell of a time stoppin' the bleedin'."

"You mustn't let me bleed any more."

"How about—that splintered bone?"

"You'll saw it off above the break where it's smashed."

"Saw! We haven't anythin' but the big crosscut saw. It'd be impossible to use that."

"There's a three-cornered file we brought to sharpen that saw. You'll make a saw out of your big huntin' knife."

"How?" burst out Jake incredulously.

"File the back of it into sharp saw teeth."

"Reckon I might," muttered Jake doubtfully. Still the idea was sinking in. "But even if I . . . Verde, you forget the worst danger."

"Boy, this is my leg an' my life. You can gamble I'm not forgettin' anythin'!"

"But blood poisonin'! . . . That couldn't be prevented. We've nothin' to—"

"Wrong. We've got fire!" flashed Verde.

Jake stared at him, dominated by Verde's tremendous force.

"Fire?" he echoed.

"Listen. You're sure thick-headed. All we got to do is plan it right—then work fast. My job is to bear it—yours to make it a clean, quick one. . . . You'll sharpen both our huntin' knives. Sharp as razors. You'll file the back of the long blade into a saw. Then you'll scour a pot an' heat water to boilin'. You'll put the knives in that. Then you'll have your straight brandin' iron in the fire. It must be red hot. Shore you know how slick you are with a brandin' iron? . . . Wal, now. You'll make sure where to cut my leg above the mashed place. You'll bind it tight, so it cain't bleed. Then when all's ready you'll cut the flesh all around, quick an' clean, clear to the bone. Then you'll saw through the bone. Then you'll grab your red-hot brandin' iron an' burn the stub across. That'll sear bone an' arteries an' flesh. You'll loosen the cord, an' wrap up my leg in a clean towel or shirt. . . . An' that's all."

"That's all!" blazed Jake. "Good Gawd, Verde! . . . Can you stand it?"

"I can an' will, old boy. I reckon it'll not be as bad as we think. For there's not much feelin' left in that leg."

"When?" gasped Jake. The excitement of the idea had gripped him. The thought that there might still be a chance to save Verde's life was all-consuming.

"Right now!" replied Verde. He had convinced Jake to undertake the terrible responsibility! Convinced him by persuasion, and in the end by falsehood, because during the excitement of this discussion the numbed leg had revived to exquisite pain. But Verde swore in his soul that he would endure and live.

Jake became actuated by supreme, uplifting, galvanizing hope. He was a changed man. Swiftly, quick and hard, he went at the preliminary tasks. He built a roaring fire. He scoured a big iron pot until it shone. He filled it with water and put it on to boil. He scraped all the rust off the branding iron, gave it a polish, and then thrust it in the heart of the red coals. Next he sharpened the knives, and filed the back of the blade of the long one. He was deft and sure, absorbed in each task. It took a long time to notch the blade into a saw and to sharpen the notches, but at last he was satisfied.

"Let me see it, Jake," asked Verde.

It was a ten-inch blade, worn thin from use. Verde felt the sharp teeth.

"Wal, Jake, that'll do the trick pronto," said Verde as coolly as if it was the bone of a horse or steer they were talking about.

"Lucky I've some clean soft shirts," returned Jake. "Ma put them in my bag."

"Good. Tear one up into strips."

"Now what next?" asked Jake, rolling up his sleeves.

"You'll want my leg on somethin' solid. Knock off the top of the bench."

Jake did so, and stripping off the blanket that covered Verde he slipped the board under his shattered leg.

"Verde, ought I to tie you?" asked Jake in solemn earnestness.

"No, Jake, I'll not make a fuss. Don't worry about me. Just you have everythin' ready—then be quick. Make it a clean job. Savvy?"

"I'll have it off quicker'n you can say Jack Robinson," replied Jake.

The boyhood term, used so unconsciously, recalled to Verde a faraway past.

A ponderous blackness seemed to float slowly before Verde's sight. The cabin was dim, vague, like the unreality of a dream.

He lay like a stone, with no power to move, yet his body seemed aquiver in a mighty convulsion of nerves—a million shocks of agony that ranged through him. A tremendous current swelled and burned in his marrow, like a boring worm of fire, up his spine, into his brain.

8

IT WAS NIGHT, AND OUTSIDE THE STORM
moaned and wailed and raged. The shadows cast by the fire flickered their last;
the red glow of the dying embers faded.

Jake had fallen into the sleep of exhaustion.

But Verde was hovering on the verge of
a great and eternal sleep. He knew that
death for him was very close. He felt the
cool sweet winds of oblivion; he saw the
wide, vacant, naked hallway of the beyond, the dim, mystic spiritland; he heard
the strange alluring voices. He had only
to let go. And every atom of his racked

body clamored to be freed. But Verde held on.

It came a thousand times—that wraith-like presence, the specter that contended with Verde's unquenchable will. And then it came no more.

One morning Verde awoke from a deep slumber that had followed his night of agony.

The storm was over. A marble-white and glistening world of snow shone dazzlingly bright from the cabin doorway. Verde heard the sharp ringing of an ax. He saw that one end of the cabin was neatly stacked with firewood. A cheerful blaze crackled on the hearth.

Verde felt a surge of life within him. The crisis was past. The pangs of his poor maimed body were innumerable; but the great rending torture had ebbed and passed away.

Jake entered to greet him with a glad shout.

Another day Verde began to take nourishment that Jake most carefully prepared, and sparingly doled out.

"Shore you're hungry," he agreed, with his eager smile. "But I cain't let you eat much yet. An' for that matter we're both goin' to get good an' damn hungry before the snow melts."

"Reckon I forgot," replied Verde in his weak voice. "How are we fixed for grub?"

"Pretty darn lucky," said Jake fervently. "We always packed up more canned stuff than we ever used. An' there's a lot, some fruit an' milk, but most vegetables. There's a sack of flour an' a couple sacks of beans. Coffee not a great deal, but lots of sugar. There's a hundred pounds of salt that I packed up last spring to cure hides. Lucky that was! An' I've hung up three deer I shot, an' one of my horses. The meat's froze solid. An' I guess that's all."

"Pretty lucky, yes," replied Verde. "But it's a long way from enough. Let's see— what's the date?"

"I don't know exactly. It's well on in November. I'll keep track of days."

"We're snowed up for five months."

"Wal, Verde, it seemed turrible at furst, before I felt shore of you comin' round, but it doesn't faze me now."

"All the same, old boy, it's far the biggest job you ever tackled," replied Verde.

"Reckon so. But don't you worry," said Jake reassuringly. "We'll go easy with our grub. I always was a meat eater, you know, an' I can live on meat. I'll find my other horse an' kill him. Then I saw elk tracks up the canyon, but I didn't want to take time to trail them. I'll do it soon. No, I'm more worried about scarcity of wood than meat. You see there's a couple of feet of snow on, an' down timber is hard to locate."

"The avalanche must have fetched down more wood than we'll need."

"Shore," said Jake, slapping his leg. "I never thought of that. Reckon I sort of shunned the avalanche end of our prison. But with lots of wood I can beat this game."

Verde noted that from this time on Jake was outdoors most of the daylight hours. To be sure, the days were short. But Verde soon became convinced that dry wood and fresh meat were harder to procure than Jake had acknowledged.

Jake ministered to Verde's comfort and health with the care of a mother. Indeed, as days went by he grew more tender in his ministrations; and as Verde's pain lessened and he showed signs of renewing strength, Jake's unspoken worry lessened and he grew happy.

It dawned upon Verde, after a while, that Jake was happier than he had ever been, even before Kitty Mains had come into their lives. Verde guessed at the first flush of this discovery that Jake's happiness came from having saved him, and from the daily service the situation made imperative. But after a while Verde altered this conviction, and arrived at the conclusion that it came from a revival of Jake's earlier love for him. Anyway, Jake's care of him was very sure and very beautiful. Verde never ceased to thank God that he had made the superhuman fight to hold on to life. It had been solely for Jake's sake, but now he began to be glad for his own. He knew that he would manage somehow to ride a horse again.

One night after supper, with the cabin warm and cozy in the firelight and the snow pattering again against the walls, Jake sat a long time staring into the fire. Every once in a while he would throw on a few chips. Finally he turned a changed and softened face to Verde—a face that revealed a beautiful, strange smile and a warm light in his eyes.

"Verde, I reckon it's no exaggeration to say you're out of danger. Your leg has healed. You're on the mend."

"Yes, thanks to you, old boy," returned Verde gratefully.

"Well, you can thank me all you like, but I'm thankin' Gawd. . . . An', Verde, are you forgettin' how you come to be here in this shape?"

"Reckon I am, now you make me think."

Jake paused to moisten his lips, and his big hand smoothed his long hair.

"I hope you can forgive me, Verde."

"There's nothing to forgive. I'm as much to blame as you. An' mebbe more."

"Wal, we won't argue thet. . . . Do you ever think of Kitty Mains?"

"Shore I do—a lot. When I cain't help myself."

"Verde, you loved Kitty somethin' turrible, didn't you?"

"I'm afraid I did."

"But you do—yet?" demanded Jake intensely, as if any intimation otherwise would be sacrilege.

"All right. Yes, I do yet," replied Verde, hastening to help Jake to his revelation, whatever it was to be.

"Shore, I'm glad. It wouldn't be fair to Kitty if our—our differences an' this trouble made you love her less. Because, Verde—I know Kitty loved you more than me."

"How do you know that?" asked Verde curiously.

"I reckon I found it out thinkin'. Somethin' came to me lyin' there awake so many nights. An' it was this. Kitty has two natures same as she has eyes. Now I was always easy with girls. Guess I must have a little of girl nature in me. Anyway my coaxin' an' tender kind of love appealed to Kitty's softer side. But that side wasn't Kitty's deepest an' strongest. She's more devil than angel, you can bet. She'd need to be tamed, an' I never could do it. She'd soon tire of me. . . . I always saw how Kitty flared up when you came around. If I'd have been honest with myself I'd of known what it meant. But I never knew until that night of the last dance. It nearly killed me then, but I've lived to be glad. . . . Verde, I reckon mebbe Kitty isn't all you an' I dreamed she was. But she is what she is an' we both love her. Now since we've been here alone I've reasoned it all out. Mebbe Kitty really does love you best. She ought to, you're so handsome, Verde. So I'm givin' up my share in her to you."

"But, Jake—" began Verde feebly.

"There's not any buts," interrupted Jake. "I've settled it. I know I'm right. An' I know this will help you to get well an' strong quicker'n anythin' else in the world."

Verde closed his eyes. He was troubled and shaken, and yet glad to have any expostulation on his part so summarily dismissed. But he knew in his heart that he had not accepted Jake's ultimatum, and that a tremendous issue still loomed in the vague future. Just now he discovered how weak he was, both physically and spiritually. It was good to sink down—to realize that slumber would come. Good old Jake! ... Verde was a little boy again, wandering along the road. He came to a stream where the water ran swiftly and the leaves floated down. The white sycamore trees stood up like ghosts. He did not want to go back to the wagon, for his stepfather hated him and beat him. . . . He was lost and he began to be afraid. Then a barefooted boy came out of the brush. "My name's Jake," the boy said. "What's yours?" And craftily he would not tell because he wished to stay.

9

THE DEAD, COLD WHITE WINTER SHUT DOWN upon Black Gorge. The short days and the long nights passed. Verde slept most of the time. Jake labored at his tasks. Sometimes after supper he would play checkers with Verde on a rude board of his own construction. Or they held council over the all-important speculations of when and how they would dare attempt to get out of the gorge. Or more often they talked over the nearer and more serious problem of fighting the cold and starvation. They never mentioned Kitty Mains. Jake's peace and serenity had somehow been communicated to Verde.

It was a wonderful occasion for both when Verde rose from his bed and hobbled about the cabin on the crutch Jake had made. From that day Verde's progress grew more rapid. He looked forward to the supreme test that was to come—the climbing out of the canyon. He wanted to be able to help himself again. Jake had become a gaunt bearded giant, hardy as a pine.

It was true that he could thrive on a meat diet. But their meat was dwindling, and if Jake did not soon make a lucky stalk their supply would be exhausted and they must face starvation. Every day Jake hunted in the recesses of the winding gorge. Several times he had been on the eve of sighting elk, but the advent of night and fresh snow covering the tracks each time had frustrated his hopes.

The days passed, and the hours of sunlight lengthened. The snow melted from the cabin roof and then disappeared from the south slope of the gorge. The icy clutch of winter loosened. Sometimes a warm, balmy breath of wind came wandering through the depths of the gorge.

With spring close at hand they came to the last pound of meat and the last hard biscuit each. Jake, giant that he was, had lately grown much gaunter. He had been sacrificing his food for Verde. When Verde discovered this he refused to eat at all unless Jake had an equal share. So they cooked the last pound of frozen meat.

Then Jake left with his rifle. Verde could now manage very well with his crutch. He did the chores while Jake hunted. There was a beautiful sky that afternoon. Verde gazed up wistfully over the pink-tinged snow ridges. Spring was coming. What a winter Jake and he had put in! Yet Verde would not have wanted it different, even to the recovery of his leg. Jake's labors had been as great as his own sufferings. Together they had conquered something more fearful than death. Together they had climbed heights more beautiful than life itself.

Before the sunset flush had paled on the high ridges Jake came staggering in under a load of meat. With a heavy crash he threw down a haunch of elk. He was covered with snow and blood. A pungent animal odor and the scent of the woods emanated from him to fill the cabin.

"Killed a bull an' a yearlin'," he boomed, with his deep-set eyes beaming gladly upon Verde. "They've been hidin' from me all winter. But I found them. . . . An'

Verde, soon I'll be makin' a sled to haul you home."

"Say, you great big ragamuffin!" yelled Verde with a joy that matched Jake's own. "I'll walk home on one leg!"

Jake had the impetuosity to make the start soon, but Verde had the wisdom and courage to wait awhile longer. The fresh meat would build up their strength and the longer they delayed the less snow they would have to combat.

During these last days Jake cut a zigzag trail in the snow up the side of the avalanche. This side, being on the north, did not get the sun except for a brief while each day. The obstacle that imprisoned them, however, was the deep snow on top. Jake climbed high enough to see that the south slopes everywhere showed great patches of black where it had thawed. He was jubilant.

"Verde, I'm rarin' to go. Once on top the rest will be easy!"

The night before the day they meant to undertake the climb upon which so much depended, Verde came out with something that had for long obsessed his mind, and had been greatly contributary to the source of his own tranquility.

"Wal, Jake, now it's time to get somethin' off my own chest," he said, with all the calmness he could muster.

"Ahuh?" asked Jake rather sharply. Evidently he did not like Verde's look.

"I didn't say so before, but I never agreed with you on that deal about Kitty Mains."

"No! ... Say, ain't it kinda late in the day to—"

"Late, but better than never.... Jake, old boy, I cain't accept what you wanted. I never agreed with you. An' I simply won't let you give up Kitty for me."

Jake turned red under his matted beard. He left off the task in hand and stood up to confront Verde.

"Don't you love Kitty same as I do?" he demanded.

Verde had his argument all planned, and the fact that in some degree it departed from strict veracity caused him no concern.

"Wal, I reckon I did once, but hardly now. This winter has knocked a lot out of me. Then I'm a cripple now, an' I never saw thet women cared a heap for cripples, except with a sort of pity. I cain't work as I used to, an' I'll be dependent upon your pa.... Jake, he's been a dad to me, same as you've been a brother, Gawd bless you! But after all my name's not

Dunton. I haven't any real name to give a woman. . . . Now all these things helped me to make up my mind. Fust an' last though, the biggest reason is that no matter what you say against it, I believe Kitty loves you best."

"Verde, you're a doggone liar!" declared Jake huskily.

"Well, if she didn't last fall, it's a shore bet she will now. I'm only half a man, Jake. . . . So let's shake hands on it."

"What if I won't?"

"I'd hate to say, Jake. Fact is, I don't know. Because my thinkin' didn't get so far. I might never leave this cabin with you. . . . See it my way, Jake. You got to! We've come through hell, an' we're happy in spite of it—perhaps because of it. I don't know. Only I'd never be happy again if you won't take it my way."

Jake wrung Verde's hand, and turned away, mute and shaken, his head bowed.

Next morning at sunrise they started. Verde had only his crutch. Jake had a blanket strapped to his back, and he carried some strips of cooked meat in his pocket and a rope in his hand. He had carried the sled high up on the slope to use in case the snow was not gone from the ridge top and the south slope beyond.

The plan was to climb very slowly, foot by foot, to husband Verde's strength. Two things became manifest during the early hours of the ascent—first, that the difficulties were greater than they had anticipated, and secondly that Verde had amazing strength and endurance.

But he gave out before they reached the top. Whereupon Jake took Verde over his shoulder, and carried him as he would a sack of meal. All winter Jake had packed heavy logs down to the cabin—packed them when he might have cut them into lesser lengths. But he had looked far ahead—to this terrible ascent out of Black Gorge. He was indeed a giant. Verde marveled at him. On the other hand, he was as slow and cautious as he was powerful and enduring. He carried Verde for only short distances, sometimes only a few yards. Then he would lower him to his foot and crutch on some high place. Thus, when he had caught his breath again, he would not have to bend down and lift Verde.

Up and up he toiled. The real Herculean labor began at the end of the trail Jake had cut in the snow. Verde almost despaired. But he could not flinch in the face of this magnificent and invincible courage. Jake had meant to kill him once and now he meant to save him. It was written. Verde felt it. And when his reason argued that Jake must soon fall broken and spent something told him no physical obstacle could conquer this man.

The afternoon waned. Sunset found them in deep snow. But before night came Jake had dragged Verde over the top of the ridge and down onto bare ground. There he fell, gasping and voiceless.

Verde set about gathering dead brush, which he piled in the lee of a large rock. Jake came presently, and helped him build a roaring fire. Then they heated the strips of meat and ate them. Jake cut spruce boughs and made a bed of them between the fire and the rock. Verde lay warm under the blanket, but he could not go to sleep immediately. Jake hunched close to the fire. His heart was too full for words, or sleep, or anything but a silent realization of deliverance and happiness.

The night wind moaned, but not with the moan of winter.

Sunrise found them on their way down the vast slope of brown and green which was dotted with patches of snow. The descent was easy, though slow. They had only to thread their way between the unthawed drifts and the thickets of brush. For a lodestone of hope they had their first sight of the Dunton ranch, a tiny green grass plot far in the distance, but coming even closer.

Again sunset burned red and gold in the sky. Verde could now gaze back and up at the rim, bold and beautiful with its belt of bright-colored cliffs and its fringed line of black pines.

With Jake's arm upholding Verde, they staggered across the ranch field, to encounter Dunton coming out of the cabin. He dropped a bucket he had been carrying.

"Jane—wife—come quick!" he yelled.

Jake waved a tired hand.

"Dad, it's me an' Verde!"

"My Gawd! You infernal scarecrows!"

Then the mother came, white-faced, to scream a wondering, ecstatic welcome.

The warm, bright living room seemed like heaven to Verde. He could only look and feel, as he lay back, propped in a comfortable rocking chair, How good to be home! That wild, white mantled gorge retreated from his memory.

It was Jake who talked, who laughed when his mother wept.

Dunton cast eyes both happy and sad over his returned sons.

"So thet's your story," he said. "Wal, the Tonto never heard its beat. I reckon

I'm proud of you both. . . . But, my Gawd,
boys, the pity of it! . . . And fer nothin'!
All for a slip of a popeyed girl who wasn't
worth your little finger, let alone a leg!
Shore! Folks hadn't even stopped talkin'
about your fight when she up an' married
young Stillwell."

THE KIDNAPPING
OF ROSETA UVALDO

1

PERIODICALLY OF LATE, ESPECIALLY AFTER
some bloody affray or other, Vaughn Medill, ranger of Texas, suffered from spells
of depression and longing for a ranch and
wife and children. The fact that few rangers ever attained these cherished posses-
sions did not detract from their appeal.
At such times the long service to his great
state, which owed so much to the rangers,
was apt to lose its importance.

Vaughn sat in the shade of the adobe
house, on the bank of the slow-eddying,
muddy Rio Grande, outside the town of
Brownsville. He was alone at this ranger
headquarters for the very good reason

that his chief, Captain Allerton, and two comrades were laid up in the hospital. Vaughn, with his usual notorious luck, had come out of the Cutter rustling fight without a scratch.

He had needed a few days off, to go alone into the mountains and there get rid of the sickness killing always engendered in him. No wonder he got red in the face and swore when some admiring tourist asked him how many men he had killed. Vaughn had been long in the service. Like other Texas youths he had enlisted in this famous and unique state constabulary before he was twenty, and he refused to count the years he had served. He had the stature of the born Texan. And the lined, weathered face, the resolute lips, grim except when he smiled, and the narrowed eyes of cool gray, and the tinge of white over his temples did not begin to tell the truth about his age.

Vaughn watched the yellow river that separated his state from Mexico. He had reason to hate that strip of dirty water and the hot mosquito and cactus land beyond. Like as not, this very day or tomorrow he would have to go across and arrest some renegade native or fetch back a stolen calf or shoot it out with Quinola and his band, who were known to be on American soil again. Vaughn shared in common with all Texans a supreme contempt for people who were so unfortunate as to live south of the border. His father had been a soldier in both Texas wars, and Vaughn had inherited his conviction that all Mexicans were his natural enemies. He knew this was not really true. Villa was an old acquaintance, and he had listed among men to whom he owed his life, Martiniano, one of the greatest of the Texas *vaqueros.*

Brooding never got Vaughn anywhere, except into deeper melancholy. This drowsy summer day he got in very deep indeed, so deep that he began to mourn over the several girls he might—at least he believed he might—have married. It all seemed so long ago, when he was on fire with the ranger spirit and would not have sacrificed any girl to the agony of waiting for her ranger to come home—knowing that some day he would never come again. Since then sentimental affairs of the heart had been few and far between; and the very latest, dating to this very hour, concerned Roseta, daughter of Uvaldo, foreman for the big Glover ranch just down the river.

Uvaldo was a Mexican of quality, claiming descent from the Spanish soldier of that name. He had an American wife, owned many head of stock, and in fact was partner with Glover in several cattle deals. The black-eyed Roseta, his daughter, had been born on the American side of the river, and had shared advantages of school and contact, seldom the lot of most señoritas.

Vaughn ruminated over these few facts as the excuse for his infatuation. For a Texas ranger to fall in love with an ordinary Mexican girl was unthinkable. To be sure, it had happened, but it was something not to think about. Roseta, however, was extraordinary. She was pretty, and slight of stature—so slight that Vaughn felt ludicrous, despite his bliss, while dancing with her. If he had stretched out his long arm and she had walked under it, he would have had to lower his hand considerably to touch her glossy black head. She was roguish and coquettish, yet had the pride of her Spanish forebears. Lastly she was young, rich, the belle of Las Animas, and the despair of cowboy and *vaquero* alike.

When Vaughn had descended to the depths of his brooding he discovered, as he had many times before, that there were but slight grounds for any hopes which he may have had of winning the beautiful Roseta. The sweetness of a haunting dream was all that could be his. Only this time it seemed to hurt more. He should not have let himself in for such a catastrophe. But as he groaned in spirit and bewailed his lonely state, he could not help recalling Roseta's smiles, her favors of dances when scores of admirers were thronging after her, and the way she would single him out on those occasions. *"Un señor grande,"* she had called him, and likewise "handsome gringo," and once, with mystery and fire in her sloe-black eyes, "You Texas ranger—you bloody gunman—killer of Mexicans!"

Flirt Roseta was, of course, and doubly dangerous by reason of her mixed blood, her Spanish lineage, and her American upbringing. Uvaldo had been quoted as saying he would never let his daughter marry across the Rio Grande. Some rich rancher's son would have her hand bestowed upon him; maybe young Glover would be the lucky one. It was madness for Vaughn even to have dreamed of winning her. Yet there still abided that much youth in him.

Sounds of wheels and hoofs interrupted the ranger's reverie. He listened. A buggy had stopped out in front.

Vaughn got up and looked round the corner of the house. It was significant that he instinctively stepped out sideways, his right hand low where the heavy gun sheath hung. A ranger never presented his full front to possible bullets; it was a trick of old hands in the service.

Someone was helping a man out of the buggy. Presently Vaughn recognized Colville, a ranger comrade, who came in assisted, limping, and with his arm in a sling.

"How are you, Bill?" asked Vaughn solicitously, as he helped the driver lead Colville into the large whitewashed room.

"All right—fine, in fact, only a—little light-headed," panted the other. "Lost a sight of blood."

"You look it. Reckon you'd have done better to stay at the hospital."

"Medill, there ain't half enough rangers to go—round," replied Colville. "Cap Allerton is hurt bad—but he'll recover. An' he thought so long as I could wag I'd better come back to headquarters."

"Ahuh. What's up, Bill?" asked the ranger quietly. He really did not need to ask.

"Shore I don't know. Somethin' to do with Quinela," replied Colville. "Help me out of my coat. It's hot an' dusty. . . . Fetch me a cold drink."

"Bill, you should have stayed in town if it's ice you want," said Vaughn as he filled a dipper from the water bucket. "Haven't I run this shebang many a time?"

"Medill, you're slated for a run across the Rio—if I don't miss my guess."

"Hell you say! Alone?"

"How else, unless the rest of our outfit rides in from the Brazos. . . . Anyway, don't they call you the 'lone star ranger'? Haw! Haw!"

"Shore you don't have a hunch what's up?" inquired Vaughn again.

"Honest I don't. Allerton had to wait for more information. Then he'll send instructions. But we know Quinela was hangin' round, with some deviltry afoot."

"Bill, that bandit outfit is plumb bold these days," said Vaughn reflectively. "I wonder now."

"We're all guessin'. But Allerton swears Quinela is daid set on revenge. Lopez was some relation, we heah from Mexicans on this side. An' when we busted up Lopez' gang, we riled Quinela. He's laid that to you, Vaughn."

"Nonsense," blurted out Vaughn. "Qui-

nela has another raid on hand, or some
other thievery job of his own."

"But didn't you kill Lopez?" asked
Colville.

"I shore didn't," declared Vaughn tes-
tily. "Reckon I was there when it happened, but Lord! I wasn't the only
ranger."

"Wal, you've got the name of it an'
that's jist as bad. Not that it makes
much difference. You're used to bein'
laid for. But I reckon Cap wanted to tip
you off."

"Ahuh . . . Say, Bill," continued Vaughn,
dropping his head. "I'm shore tired of this
ranger game."

"My Gawd, who ain't! But, Vaughn, *you*
couldn't lay down on Captain Allerton
right now."

"No. but I've a notion to resign when he
gets well an' the boys come back from the
Brazos."

"An' that'd be all right, Vaughn, al-
though we'd hate to lose you," returned
Colville earnestly. "We all know—in fact
everybody who has followed the ranger
service knows you should have been a
captain long ago. But them pig-headed officials at Houston! Vaughn, your gun record—the very name an' skill that make

you a great ranger—have operated against you there."

"Reckon so. But I never wanted particularly to be a captain—leastways of late years," replied Vaughn moodily. "I'm just tired of bein' eternally on my guard. Lookin' to be shot at from every corner or bush! Think what an awful thing it was—when I near killed one of my good friends—all because he came suddenlike out of a door, pullin' at his handkerchief!"

"It's the price we pay. Texas could never have been settled at all but for the buffalo hunters first, an' then us rangers. We don't get much credit, Vaughn. But we know someday our service will be appreciated. . . . In your case everythin' is magnified. Suppose you did quit the service? Wouldn't you still stand most the same risk? Wouldn't you need to be on your guard, sleepin' an' wakin'?"

"Wal, I suppose so, for a time. But somehow I'd be relieved."

"Vaughn, the men who are lookin' for you now will always be lookin', until they're daid."

"Shore. But, Bill, that class of men don't live long on the Texas border."

"Hell! Look at Wes Hardin', Kingfisher,

Poggin—gunmen that took a long time to kill. An' look at Cortina, at Quinela—an' Villa. . . . Nope, I reckon it's the obscure relations an' friends of men you've shot that you have most to fear. An' you never know who an' where they are. It's my belief you'd be shore of longer life by stickin' to the rangers."

"Couldn't I get married an' go way off somewhere?" asked Vaughn belligerently.

Colville whistled in surprise, and then laughed. "Ahuh? So that's the lay of the land? A gal!— Wal, if the Texas ranger service is to suffer, let it be for that one cause."

Toward evening a messenger brought a letter from Captain Allerton, with the information that a drove of horses had been driven across the river west of Brownsville, at Rock Ford. They were in the charge of Mexicans and presumably had been stolen from some ranch inland. The raid could be laid to Quinela, though there was no proof of it. It bore his brand. Medill's instructions were to take the rangers and recover the horses.

"Reckon Cap thinks the boys have got back from the Brazos or he's had word they're comin'," commented Colville. "Wish I was able to ride. We wouldn't wait."

Vaughn scanned the short letter again and then filed it away among a stack of others.

"Strange business this ranger service," he said ponderingly. "Horses stolen— fetch them back! Cattle raid—recover stock! Drunken cowboy shootin' up the town—arrest him! Bandits looted the San Tone stage—fetch them in! Little Tom, Dick, or Harry lost—find him! Farmer murdered—string up the murderer!"

"Wal, come to think about it, you're right," replied Colville. "But the rangers have been doin' it for thirty or forty years. You cain't help havin' pride in the service, Medill. Half the job's done when these hombres find a ranger's on the trail. That's reputation. But I'm bound to admit the thing is strange an' shore couldn't happen nowhere else but in Texas."

"Reckon I'd better ride up to Rock Ford an' have a look at that trail."

"Wal, I'd wait till mawnin'. Mebbe the boys will come in. An' there's no sense in ridin' it twice."

* * *

The following morning after breakfast Vaughn went out to the alfalfa pasture to fetch in his horse. Next to his gun a ranger's horse was his most valuable asset. Indeed a horse often saved a ranger's life when a gun could not. Star was a big-boned chestnut, not handsome except in regard to his size, but for speed and endurance Vaughn had never owned his like. They had been on some hard jaunts together. Vaughn fetched Star into the shed and saddled him.

Presently Vaughn heard Colville shout, and upon hurrying out he saw a horseman ride furiously away from the house. Colville stood in the door waving.

Vaughn soon reached him. "Who was that feller?"

"Glover's man, Uvaldo. You know him."

"Uvaldo!" exclaimed Vaughn, startled. "He shore was in a hurry. What'd he want?"

"Captain Allerton, an' in fact all the rangers in Texas. I told Uvaldo I'd send you down pronto. He wouldn't wait. Shore was mighty excited."

"What's wrong with him?"

"His gal is gone."

"Gone!"

"Shore. He cain't say whether she eloped or was kidnapped. But it's a job for you, old man. Haw! Haw!"

"Yes, it would be—if she eloped," replied Vaughn constrainedly. "An' I reckon not a bit funny, Bill."

"Wal, hop to it," replied Colville, turning to go into the house.

Vaughn mounted his horse and spurred him into the road.

2

VAUGHN'S PERSONAL OPINION, BEFORE HE AR-
rived at Glover's ranch, was that Roseta
Uvaldo had eloped, and probably with a
cowboy or some *vaquero* with whom her
father had forbidden her to associate. In
some aspects Roseta resembled the vain
daughter of a proud don; in the main, she
was American bred and educated. But she
had that strain of blood which might well
have burned secretly to break the bonds
of conventionality. Uvaldo, himself, had
been a *vaquero* in his youth. Any Texan
could have guessed this seeing Uvaldo
ride a horse.

There was much excitement in the

Uvaldo household. Vaughn could not get any clue out of the weeping kin folks, except that Roseta had slept in her bed, and had risen early to take her morning horseback ride. All Mexicans were of a highly excitable temperament, and Uvaldo was no exception. Vaughn could not get much out of him. Roseta had not been permitted to ride off the ranch, which was something that surprised Vaughn. She was not allowed to go anywhere unaccompanied. This certainly was a departure from the freedom accorded Texan girls; nevertheless any girl of good sense would give the river a wide berth.

"Did she ride out alone?" asked Vaughn, in his slow Spanish, thinking he could get at Uvaldo better in his own tongue.

"Yes, señor. Pedro saddled her horse. No one else saw her."

"What time this morning?"

"Before sunrise."

Vaughn questioned the lean, dark *vaquero* about what clothes the girl was wearing and how she had looked and acted. The answer was that Roseta had dressed in *vaquero* garb, looked very pretty and full of the devil. Vaughn reflected that this was quite easy to believe. Next he questioned the stable boys and other *vaqueros* about the place. Then he rode out to the Glover ranch house and got hold of some of the cowboys, and lastly young Glover himself. Nothing further was elicited from them, except that this same thing had happened before. Vaughn hurried back to Uvaldo's house.

He had been a ranger for fifteen years and that meant a vast experience in Texas border life. It had become a part of his business to look through people. Not often was Vaughn deceived when he put a query and bent his gaze upon a man. Women, of course, were different. Uvaldo himself was the only one here who roused a doubt in Vaughn's mind. This Americanized Mexican had a terrible fear which he did not realize that he was betraying. Vaughn conceived the impression that Uvaldo had an enemy and he had only to ask him if he knew Quinela to get on the track of something. Uvaldo was probably lying when he professed fear that Roseta had eloped.

"You think she ran off with a cowboy or some young feller from town?" inquired Vaughn.

"No, señor. With a *vaquero* or a peon," came the amazing reply.

Vaughn gave up here, seeing he was losing time.

"Pedro, show me Roseta's horse tracks," he requested.

"Señor, I will give you ten thousand dollars if you bring my daughter back—alive," said Uvaldo.

"Rangers don't accept money for their services," replied Vaughn briefly, further mystified by the Mexican's intimation that Roseta might be in danger of foul play. "I'll fetch her back—one way or another—unless she has eloped. If she's gotten married I can do nothin'."

Pedro showed the ranger the small hoof tracks made by Roseta's horse. He studied them a few moments, and then, motioning those following him to stay back, he led his own horse and walked out of the courtyard, down the lane, through the open gate, and into the field.

Every boy born on the open range of vast Texas had been a horse tracker from the time he could walk. Vaughn was a past master at this cowboy art, long before he joined the rangers, and years of man-hunting had perfected it. He could read a fugitive's mind by the tracks he left in dust or sand.

He rode across Glover's broad acres, through the pecans, to where the ranch bordered on the desert. Roseta had not been bent on an aimless morning ride.

Under a clump of trees someone had waited for her. Here Vaughn dismounted to study tracks. A mettlesome horse had been tethered to one tree. In the dust were imprints of a riding boot, not the kind left by cowboy or *vaquero*. Heel and toe were broad. He found the butt of a cigarette smoked that morning. Roseta's clandestine friend was not a Mexican, much less a peon or *vaquero*. There were signs that he probably had waited there on other mornings.

Vaughn got back on his horse, strengthened in the elopement theory, though not yet wholly convinced. Maybe Roseta was just having a lark. Maybe she had a lover Uvaldo would have none of. This idea grew as Vaughn saw where the horses had walked close together, so their riders could hold hands. Perhaps more! Vaughn's silly hope oozed out and died. And he swore at his own ridiculous, vain dreams. It was all right for him to be young enough to have an infatuation for Roseta Uvaldo, but to have entertained a dream of winning her was laughable. He laughed, though mirthlessly. And jealous pangs consumed him. What an adorable, fiery creature she was! Some lucky dog from Brownsville had won her. Mingled with Vaughn's romantic feelings was one of relief.

"Reckon I'd better get back to rangerin' instead of moonin'," he thought grimly.

The tracks led in a roundabout way through the mesquite to the river trail. This was two miles or more from the line of the Glover ranch. The trail was broad and lined by trees. It was a lonely and unfrequented place for lovers to ride. Roseta and her companion still were walking their horses. On this beautiful trail, which invited a gallop or at least a canter, only love-making could account for the leisurely gait. Also the risk! Whoever Roseta's lover might be, he was either a fool or plain fearless. Vaughn swore lustily as the tracks led on and on, deeper into the timber that bordered the Rio Grande.

Suddenly Vaughn drew up sharply, with an exclamation. Then he slid out of his saddle, to bend over a marked change in the tracks he was trailing. Both horse had reared, to come down hard on forehoofs, and then jump sideways.

"By God! A holdup!" grunted Vaughn in sudden concern.

Sandal tracks in the dust! A native bandit had been hiding behind a thicket in ambush. Vaughn swiftly tracked the horses off the trail, to an open glade on the bank, where hoof tracks of other horses joined them and likewise boot tracks. Vaughn did not need to see that these new marks had been made by Mexican boots.

Roseta had either been led into a trap by the man she had met or they had both been ambushed by three Mexicans. It was a common thing along the border for Mexican marauders to kidnap Mexican girls. The instances of abduction of American girls had been few and far between, though Vaughn remembered several over the years whom he had helped to rescue. They had been pretty sorry creatures, and one was even demented. Roseta being the daughter of the rich Uvaldo, would be held for ransom and therefore she might escape the usual horrible treatment. Vaughn's sincere and honest love for Roseta made him at once annoyed with her heedless act, jealous of the unknown who had kept tryst with her, and fearful of her possible fate.

"Three hours start on me," he muttered, consulting his watch. "Reckon I can come up on them before dark."

The ranger followed the broad, fresh trail that wound down through timber and brush to the river bottom. A border of arrow weed stretched out across a sand bar. All at once he halted stock-still, then moved as if to dismount. But it was not necessary. He could read from the saddle another story in the sand and this one was one of tragedy. A round depression in the sand and one spot of reddish color, obviously blood, on the slender white stalk of arrow weed, a heavy furrow, and then a path as though made by a dragged body through the green to the river— these easily-read signs added a sinister note to the abduction of Roseta Uvaldo. In Vaughn's estimation it cleared Roseta's comrade of all complicity, except that of heedless risk. And the affair began to savor somewhat of Quinela's work. The ranger wondered whether Quinela, the mere mention of whose name had brought a look of terror into Uvaldo's eyes when Vaughn had spoken to him, might not be a greater menace than the Americans believed. If so, then God help Roseta!

Vaughn took time enough to dismount and trail the path through the weeds where the murderers had dragged the body. They had been bold and careless. Vaughn picked up a cigarette case, a glove, and a watch, and he made sure that by the latter he could identify Roseta's companion on this fatal ride. A point of gravel led out to a deep current in the river, to which the body had been consigned. It might be several days and many miles below where the Rio Grande would give up its dead.

The exigencies of the case prevented Vaughn from going back after food and canteen. Many a time had he been caught in the same predicament. He had only his horse, a gun, and a belt full of cartridges. But they were sufficient for the job that lay ahead of him.

Hurrying back to Star he led him along the trail to the point where the Mexicans had gone into the river. The Rio was treacherous with quicksand, but it was always safe to follow Mexicans, provided one could imitate them. Vaughn spurred his horse across the oozy sand, and made deep water just in the nick of time. The swift current, however, was nothing for the powerful Star to breast. Vaughn emerged at precisely the point where the Mexicans had climbed out, but to help Star he threw himself forward, and catching some arrow weeks, hauled himself up the steep bank. Star floundered out and plunged up to solid ground.

The ranger mounted again and took the trail without any concern of being ambushed. Three Mexicans bent on a desperate deal of this sort would not hang back on the trail to wait for pursuers. Once up the level mesquite land it was plain that they had traveled at a brisk trot. Vaughn loped Star along the well-defined tracks of five horses. At this gait he felt sure that he was covering two miles while they were traveling one. He calculated that they should be about fifteen miles ahead of him, unless rough country had slowed them, and that by early afternoon he ought to be close on their heels. If their trail had worked down the river toward Rock Ford he might have connected these three riders with the marauders mentioned in Captain Allerton's letter. But it led straight south of the Rio Grande and showed that the kidnapers had a definite destination in mind.

Vaughn rode for two hours before he began to climb out of the level river valley. Then he struck rocky hills covered with cactus and separated by dry gorges. There was no difficulty in following the trail, but he had to proceed more slowly. He did not intend that Roseta Uvaldo should be forced to spend a night in the clutches of these desperadoes. Toward noon the sun grew hot and Vaughn began to suffer from thirst. Star was soaked with sweat, but showed no sign of distress.

He came presently to a shady spot where it was evident that the abductors had halted, probably to eat and rest. The remains of a small fire showed in a circle of stones. Vaughn got off to put his hand on the mesquite ashes. They were still hot. This meant something, though not a great deal. Mesquite wood burned slowly and the ashes retained heat for a long while. Vaughn also examined horse tracks so fresh that no particle of dust had yet blown into them. Two hours behind, perhaps a little more or less!

He resumed the pursuit, making good time everywhere, at a swift lope on all possible stretches.

There was a sameness to the brushy growth and barren hills and rocky dry ravines, though the country was growing rougher. He had not been through this section before. He crossed no trails. And he noted that the tracks of the Mexicans gradually were heading from south to west. Sooner or later they were bound to join the well-known Rock Ford trail. Vaughn was concerned about this. Should he push Star to the limit until he knew he was close behind the abductors? It would not do to let them see or hear him. If he could surprise them the thing would be easy. While he revolved these details of the problem in his mind he kept traveling full speed along the trail.

He passed an Indian corn field, and then a hut of adobe and brush. The tracks he was hounding kept straight on, and led off the desert into a road, not, however, the Rock Ford road. Vaughn here urged Star to his best speed, and a half hour later he was turning into a well-defined trail. He did not need to get off to see that no horses but the five he was tracking had passed this point since morning. Moreover, it was plain that they were not many miles ahead.

Vaughn rode on awhile at full gallop, then turning off the trail, he kept Star to that same ground-eating gait in a long detour. Once he crossed a stream bed, up which there would be water somewhere. Then he met the trail again, finding to his disappointment and chagrin that the tracks indicated that the riders had passed. He had hoped to head off the desperadoes and lie in wait for them here.

Mid-afternoon was on him. He decided not to force the issue at once. There was no ranch or village within half a night's ride of this spot. About sunset the Mexicans would halt to rest and eat. They would build a fire.

Vaughn rode down into a rocky defile

where he found a much-needed drink for himself and Star. He did not relish the winding trail ahead. It kept to the gorge. It was shady and cool, but afforded too many places where he might be ambushed. Still, there was no choice; he had to go on. He had no concern for himself that the three hombres would ambush him. But if they fell in with another band of cutthroats! It was Roseta of whom he was thinking.

Vaughn approached a rocky wall. He was inured to danger. And his ranger luck was proverbial. As he turned the corner of the rock wall he found himself facing a line of men with leveled rifles.

"Hands up, gringo ranger!"

3

Vaughn was as much surprised by the command given in English as by this totally unexpected encounter with a dozen or more Mexicans. He knew the type all too well. These were Quinela's bandits.

Vaughn raised his hands. Why this gang leader was holding him up instead of shooting on sight was beyond Vaughn's ken. The Mexicans began to jabber like a lot of angry monkeys. If ever Vaughn expected death it was at that moment. He had about decided to pull his gun and shoot it out with them, and finish as many a ranger had before him. But a shrill authoritative voice deterred him. Then a swarthy little man, lean-faced, and beady-eyed, stepped out between the threatening rifles and Vaughn. He silenced the shrill chatter of his men.

"It's the gringo ranger, Texas Medill," he shouted in Spanish. "It's the man who killed Lopez. Don't shoot. Quinela will pay much gold for him alive. Quinela will strip off the soles of his feet and drive him with hot irons to walk on the choya."

"But it's the dreaded gun ranger señor," protested a one-eyed bandit. "The only safe way is to shoot his cursed heart out here."

"We had our orders to draw this ranger across the river," returned the leader harshly. "Quinela knew his man and the hour. The Uvaldo girl brought him. And here we have him—alive! ... Garcia, it'd cost your life to shoot this ranger."

"But I warn you, Juan, he is not alone," returned Garcia. "He is but a leader of many rangers. Best kill him quick and hurry on. I have told you already that plenty gringo *vaqueros* are on the trail. We have many horses. We cannot travel fast. Night is coming. Best kill Texas Medill."

"No, Garcia. We obey orders," returned Juan harshly. "We take him alive to Quinela."

Vaughn surveyed the motley group with speculative eyes. He could kill six of them at least, and with Star charging and the poor marksmanship of native bandits, he might break through. Coldly Vaughn weighed the chances. They were a hundred to one that he would not escape. Yet he had taken such chances before. But these men had Roseta, and while there was life there was always some hope. With a tremendous effort of will he forced aside the deadly impulse and applied his wits to the situation.

The swarthy Juan turned to cover Vaughn with a cocked gun. Vaughn read doubt and fear in the beady eyes. He knew Mexicans. If they did not kill him at once there was hope. At a significant motion Vaughn carefully shifted a long leg and stepped face front, hands high, out of the saddle.

Juan addressed him in Spanish.

"No savvy, señor," replied the ranger.

"You speak Spanish?" repeated the questioner in English.

"Very little. I understand some of your Mexican lingo."

"You trailed Manuel alone?"

"Who's Manuel?"

"My *vaquero*. He brought Señorita Uvaldo across the river."

133

"After murdering her companion. Yes, I trailed him and two other men, I reckon. Five horses. The Uvaldo girl rode one. The fifth horse belonged to her companion."

"Ha! Did Manuel kill?" exclaimed the Mexican, and it was quite certain that this was news to him.

"Yes. You have murder as well as kidnapping to answer for."

The Mexican cursed under his breath.

"Where are your rangers?" he went on.

"They got back from the Brazos last night with news of your raid," said Vaughn glibly. "And this morning they joined the cowboys who were trailing the horses you stole."

Vaughn realized then that somewhere there had been a mix-up in Quinela's plans. The one concerning the kidnapping of Roseta Uvaldo and Vaughn's taking the trail had worked out well. But Juan's dark, corded face, his volley of unintelligible maledictions directed at his men betrayed a hitch somewhere. Again Vaughn felt the urge to draw and fight it out. What crazy fiery-headed fools these tattered marauders were! Juan had lowered his gun to heap abuse on Garcia. That luckless individual turned green of face. Some of the others still held leveled rifles on Vaughn, but they were looking at their leader and his lieutenant. Vaughn saw a fair chance to get away, and his gun hand itched. A heavy-booming Colt—Juan and Garcia dead—a couple of shots at those other outlaws—that would have stampeded them. But Vaughn as yet had caught no glimpse of Roseta. He put the grim, cold impulse behind him.

The harangue went on, ending only when Garcia had been cursed into sullen agreement.

"I'll take them to Quinela," cried Juan shrilly, and began shouting orders.

Vaughn's gun belt was removed. His hands were tied behind his back. He was forced upon one of the Mexicans' horses and his feet were roped to the stirrups. Juan appropriated his gun belt, which he put on with the Mexican's love of vainglory, and then mounted Star. The horse did not like the exchange of riders, and there followed immediate evidence of the cruel iron hand of the outlaw. Vaughn's blood leaped, and he veiled his eyes lest someone see his savage urge to kill. When he raised his head, two of the squat, motley-garbed, and wide-sombreroed Mexicans were riding by, and the second led a horse upon which sat Roseta Uvaldo.

She was bound to the saddle, but her hands were free. She turned her face to

Vaughn. With what concern and longing did he gaze at it! Vaughn needed only to see it flash white toward him, to meet the look of gratitude in her dark eyes, to realize that Roseta was still unharmed. She held her small proud head high. Her spirit was unbroken. For the rest, what mattered the dusty disheveled hair, the mud-spattered and dust-covered *vaquero* riding garb she wore? Vaughn flashed her a look that brought the blood to her pale cheeks.

Juan prodded Vaughn in the back. "Ride, gringo." Then he gave Garcia a last harsh command. As Vaughn's horse followed that of Roseta and her two guards into the brook, there rose a clattering, jabbering melee among the Mexicans left behind. It ended in a receding roar of pounding hoofs.

The brook was shallow and ran swiftly over gravel and rocks. Vaughn saw at once that Juan meant to hide his trail. An hour after the cavalcade would have passed a given point here, no obvious trace would show. The swift water would have cleared as well as have filled the hoof tracks with sand.

"Juan, you were wise to desert your gang of horse thieves," said Vaughn coolly. "There's a hard-ridin' outfit on their trail. And some, if not all of them, will be dead before sundown."

"*Quién sabe?* But it's sure Texas Medill will be walking choya on bare-skinned feet *mañana*," replied the Mexican bandit chief.

Vaughn pondered. Quinela's rendezvous, then, was not many hours distant. Travel such as this, up a rocky gorge, was necessarily slow. Probably this brook would not afford more than a few miles of going. Then Juan would head out on to the desert and try in other ways to hide his tracks. As far as Vaughn was concerned, whether he hid them or not made no difference. The cowboys and rangers in pursuit were but fabrications of Vaughn's to deceive the Mexicans. He knew how to work on their primitive feelings. But Vaughn poignantly realized the peril of the situation and the brevity of the time left him.

"Juan, you've got my gun," said Vaughn, his keen mind working. "You say I'll be dead in less than twenty-four hours. What's it worth to untie my hands so I can ride in comfort?"

"Señor, if you have money on you it will be mine anyway," replied the Mexican.

"I haven't any money with me. But I've got my checkbook that shows a balance of some thousands of dollars in an El Paso bank," replied Vaughn, and he turned round.

The bandit showed his gleaming white teeth in derision. "What's that to me?"

"Some thousands in gold, Juan. You can get it easily. News of my death will not get across the border very soon. I'll give you a check and a letter, which you can take to El Paso, or send by messenger."

"How much gold, Señor?" Juan asked.

"Over three thousand."

"Señor, you would bribe me into a trap. No. Juan loves the glitter and clink of your American gold, but he is no fool."

"Nothing of the sort. I'm trying to buy a little comfort in my last hours. And possibly a little kindness to the señorita there. It's worth a chance. You can send a messenger. What do you care if he shouldn't come back? You don't lose anythin'."

"No gringo can be trusted, much less Texas Medill of the rangers," replied the Mexican.

"Sure. But take a look at my checkbook. You know figures when you see them."

Juan rode abreast of Vaughn, impelled by curiosity. His beady eyes glittered.

"Inside the vest pocket," directed Vaughn. "Don't drop the pencil."

The Mexican procured the checkbook and opened it. "Señor, I know your bank," he said, vain of his ability to read, which to judge by his laborious task was limited.

"Ahuh. Well, how much balance have I left?" asked Vaughn.

"Three thousand, four hundred."

"Good. Now, Juan, you may as well get that money. I've nobody to leave it to. I'll buy a little comfort for myself—and kindness to the señorita."

"How much kindness, señor?" asked the Mexican craftily.

"That you keep your men from handlin' her rough—and soon as the ransom is paid send her back safe."

"Señor, the first I have seen to. The second is not mine to grant. Quinela will demand ransom—yes—but never will he send the señorita back."

"But I—thought—"

"Quinela was wronged by Uvaldo."

Vaughn whistled at this astounding revelation. He had divined correctly the fear Uvaldo had revealed. The situation then for Roseta was vastly more critical. Death would be merciful compared to the fate the half-breed peon Quinela would deal her. Vaughn cudgled his brains in desperation. Why had he not shot it out with these yellow desperadoes? But rage could not further Roseta's cause.

Meanwhile the horses splashed and clattered over the rocks in single file up the narrowing gorge. The steep walls were giving way to brushy slopes that let the hot sun down. Roseta looked back at Vaughn with appeal and trust—and something more in her dark eyes that tortured him.

Vaughn did not have the courage to meet her gaze, except for that fleeting moment. It was only natural that his spirits should be at a low ebb. Never in his long ranger service had he encountered such a desperate situation. More than once he had faced what seemed inevitable death, where there had seemed to be not the slightest chance to escape. Vaughn was not of a temper to give up completely. He would watch for a break till the very last second. For Roseta, however, he endured agonies. He had looked at the mutilated bodies of more than one girl victim of these bandits.

When at length the gully narrowed to a mere crack in the hill, and the water failed, Juan ordered his guards to climb a steep brush slope. There was no sign of any trail. If this brook, which they had waded to its source, led away from the road to Rock Ford, it would take days before rangers or cowboys could possibly run across it. Juan was a fox.

The slope was not easy to climb. Both Mexicans got off their horses to lead Roseta's. If Vaughn had not been tied on his saddle he would have fallen off. Eventually they reached the top, to enter a thick growth of mesquite and cactus. And before long they broke out into a trail, running, as near as Vaughn could make out, at right angles to the road and river trail. Probably it did not cross either one. Certainly the Mexicans trotted east along it as if they had little to fear from anyone traveling it.

Presently a peon came in sight astride a mustang, and leading a burro. He got by the two guards, though they crowded him into the brush. But Juan halted him, and got off Star to see what was in the pack on the burro. With an exclamation of great satisfaction he pulled out what appeared to Vaughn to be a jug or demijohn covered with wickerwork. Juan pulled out the stopper and smelled the contents.

"*Canyu!*" he said, and his white teeth gleamed. He took a drink, then smacked his lips. When the guards, who had stopped to watch, made a move to dismount he cursed them vociferously. Sullenly they slid back into their saddles. Juan stuffed the demijohn into the right saddlebag of Vaughn's saddle. Here the peon protested in a mixed dialect that Vaughn could not translate. But the meaning was obvious. Juan kicked the ragged peon's sandaled foot, and ordered him on, with a significant touch of Vaughn's big gun, which he wore so pompously. The peon lost no time riding off. Juan remounted, and directed the cavalcade to move forward.

Vaughn turned as his horse started, and again he encountered Roseta's dark intent eyes. They seemed telepathic this time, as well as filled with unutterable promise. She had read Vaughn's thought. If there were anything that had dominance in the Mexican's nature it was the cactus liquor, *canyu*. Ordinarily he was volatile, unstable as water, flint one moment and wax the next. But with the burn of *canyu* in his throat he had the substance of mist.

Vaughn felt the lift and pound of his heavy heart. He had prayed for the luck of the ranger, and lo! a peon had ridden up, packing *canyu*.

4

CANYU WAS A DISTILLATION MADE FROM THE maguey cactus, a plant similar to the century plant. The peon brewed it. But in lieu of the brew, natives often cut into the heart of a plant and sucked the juice. Vaughn had once seen a Mexican sprawled in the middle of a huge maguey, his head buried deep in the heart of it and his legs hanging limp. Upon examination he appeared to be drunk, but it developed that he was dead.

This liquor was potential fire. The lack of it made the peons surly: the possession of it made them gay. One drink changed their mental and physical world. Juan whistled after the first drink: after the second he began to sing "La Paloma." His two guards cast greedy, mean looks backward.

Almost at once the fairly brisk pace of travel that had been maintained slowed perceptibly. Vaughn began to feel more sanguine. He believed that he might be able to break the thongs that bound his wrists. As he had prayed for his ranger luck so he now prayed for anything to delay these Mexicans on the trail.

The leader Juan either wanted the *canyu* for himself or was too crafty to share it with his two men; probably both. With all three of them, the center of attention had ceased to be in Uvaldo's girl and the hated gringo ranger. It lay in that demijohn in Star's saddlebag. If a devil lurked in this white liquor for them, there was likewise for the prisoners a watching angel.

The afternoon was not far enough advanced for the sun to begin losing its heat. Shade along the trail was most inviting and welcome, but it was scarce. Huge pipelike masses of organ cactus began to vary the monotonous scenery. Vaughn saw deer, rabbits, road runners, and butcherbirds. The country was uninhabited and this trail an unfrequented one which certainly must branch into one of the several main traveled trails. Vaughn hoped the end of it still lay many miles off.

The way led into a shady rocky glen. As of one accord the horses halted, without, so far as Vaughn could see, any move or word from their riders. This was proof that the two guards in the lead had ceased to ride with the sole idea in mind of keeping to a steady gait. Vaughn drew a deep breath, as if to control his nervous feeling of suspense. No man could foretell the variety of effects of *canyu* on another, but certain it must be that something would happen soon.

Juan had mellowed considerably. A subtle change had occurred in his disposition, though he was still the watchful leader. Vaughn felt that he was now in even more peril from this Mexican than before the advent of the *canyu*. This, however, would not last long. He could only bide his time, watch and think. His luck had begun to take over. He divined it, trusted it with mounting hope.

The two guards turned their horses across the trail, blocking Roseta's horse, while Vaughn's came up alongside. If he could have stretched out his hand he could have touched Roseta. Many a time he had been thrilled and bewildered in her presence, not to say stricken speechless, but he had never felt as he did now. Roseta contrived to touch his bound foot with her stirrup, and the deliberate move made Vaughn tremble. Still he did not yet look directly down at her.

The actions of the three Mexicans were as clear to Vaughn as crystal. If he had seen one fight among Mexicans over *canyu*, he had seen a hundred. First the older of the two guards leisurely got off his horse. His wide straw sombrero hid his face, except for a peaked, yellow chin, scantily covered with black whiskers. His clothes hung in rags, and a cartridge belt was slung loosely over his left shoulder. He had left his rifle in its saddle sheath, and his only weapon was a bone-handled machete stuck in a scabbard attached to his belt.

"Juan, we are thirsty and have no water," he said. And his comrade, sitting sideways in his saddle, nodded in agreement.

"Gonzalez, one drink and no more," returned Juan, and lifted out the demijohn.

With eager cry the man tipped it to his lips. And he gulped steadily until Juan jerked it away. Then the other Mexican tumbled off his horse and eagerly besought Juan for a drink, if only one precious drop. Juan complied, but this time he did not let go of the demijohn.

Vaughn felt a touch—a gentle pressure on his knee. Roseta had laid her gloved hand there. Then he had to avert his gaze from the Mexicans.

"Oh, Vaughn, I *knew* you would come to save me," she whispered. "But they have caught you.... For God's sake, do something."

"Roseta, I reckon I can't do much, at this sitting," replied Vaughn, smiling down at her. "Are you—all right?"

"Yes, except I'm tired and my legs ache. I was frightened badly before you happened along. But now—it's terrible.... Vaughn, they are taking us to Quinela. He is a monster. My father told me so.... If you can't save me you must kill me."

"I shall save you, Roseta," he whispered low, committing himself on the altar of the luck that had never failed him. The glance she gave him then made his blood run throbbing through his veins. And he thanked the fates, since he loved her and had been given this incredible opportunity, that it had fallen to his lot to become a ranger.

Her eyes held his and there was no doubt about the warm pressure of her hand on his knee. But even during this sweet stolen moment, Vaughn had tried to attend to the argument between the three Mexicans. He heard their mingled voices, all high-pitched and angry. In another moment they would be leaping at each others' throats like dogs. Vaughn was endeavoring to think of some encouraging word for Roseta, but the ranger was replaced for the moment by the man who was revealing his heart in a long look into the small pale face, with its red, quivering lips and great dark eyes uplifted, filled with blind faith.

The sound of struggling, the trample of hoofs, a shrill cry of "Santa Maria!" and a sodden blow preceded the startling crash of a gun.

As Vaughn's horse plunged he saw Roseta's mount rear into the brush with its rider screaming, and Star lunged out of a cloud of blue smoke. A moment later Vaughn found himself tearing down the trail. He was helpless, but he squeezed the scared horse with his knees and kept calling, "Whoa there—whoa boy!"

Not for a hundred rods or more did the animal slow up. It relieved Vaughn to hear a clatter of hoofs behind him, and he turned to see Juan tearing after him in pursuit. Presently he turned out into the brush, and getting ahead of Vaughn, turned into the trail again to stop the ranger's horse. Juan proceeded to beat the horse over the head until it almost unseated Vaughn.

"Hold on, man," shouted Vaughn. "It wasn't his fault or mine. Why don't you untie my hands—if you want your nag held in?"

Juan jerked the heaving horse out of the brush and onto the trail, finally leading him back toward the scene of the shooting. But before they reached it Vaughn saw one of the guards coming with Roseta and a riderless horse. Juan grunted his satisfaction, and let them pass without a word.

Roseta seemed less disturbed and shaken than Vaughn had feared she would be. Her dilated eyes, as she passed, said as plainly as any words could have done that they now had one less enemy to contend with.

The journey was resumed. Vaughn drew a deep breath and endeavored to arrange his thoughts. The sun was still only halfway down toward the western horizon. There were hours of daylight yet! And he had an ally more deadly than bullets, more subtle than any man's wit, sharper than the tooth of a serpent.

Perhaps a quarter of an hour later, Vaughn, turning his head ever so slightly, saw, out of the corner of his eye, Juan take another drink of *canyu*. And it was a good stiff one. Vaughn thrilled as he contained himself. Presently Juan's latest act would be as if it had never been. *Canyu* was an annihilation of the past.

"Juan, I'll fall off this horse pronto," began Vaughn.

"Very good, señor. Fall off," replied Juan amiably.

"But my feet are tied to the stirrups. This horse of yours is skittish. He'll bolt and drag my brains out. If you want to take me alive to Quinela, so that he may have a fiesta while I walk choya, you'd better not let me fall off."

"S. Ranger, if you fall you fall. How can I prevent it?"

"I am damned uncomfortable with my hands tied back this way. I cain't sit straight. I'm cramped. Be a good fellow, Juan, and untie my hands."

"S. Texas Medill, if you are uncomfortable now, what will you be when you tread the fiery cactus on your naked feet?"

"But that will be short. No man lives such torture long, does he, Juan?"

"The choya kills quickly, señor."

"Juan, have you thought about the gold lying in the El Paso bank? Gold that can be yours for the ride. It will be long before my death is reported across the river. You have plenty of time to get to El Paso with my check and a letter. I can write it on a sheet of paper out of my notebook. Surely you have a friend or acquaintance in El Paso or Juarez who can identify you at the bank as Juan—whatever your name is."

"Yes, señor, I have. And my name is Juan Mendoz."

"Have you thought about what you could do with three thousand dollars? Not Mexican pesos, but real gringo gold!"

"I have not thought, señor, because I do not like to give in to dreams."

"Juan, listen. You are a fool. I know I am as good as daid. What have I been a ranger all these years for? And it's worth this gold to me to be free of this miserable cramp—and to feel that I have tried to buy some little kindness for the señorita there. She is part Mexican, Juan. She had Mexican blood in her, don't forget that. . . . Well, you are not betraying Quinela. And you will be rich. You will have my horse and saddle, if you are wise enough to keep Quinela from seeing them. You will buy silver spurs—with the long

Spanish rowels. You will have jingling gold in your pocket. You will buy a *vaquero*'s sombrero. And then think of your *chata*—your sweetheart, Juan.... Ah, I knew it. You have a *chata*. Think of what you can buy her. A Spanish mantilla, and a golden cross, and silver-buckled shoes for her little feet. Think how she will love you for that! ... Then, Juan, best of all, you can go far south of the border—buy a hacienda, horses, and cattle, and live there happily with your *chata*. You will only get killed in Quinela's service—for a few dirty pesos.... You will raise mescal on your hacienda, and brew your own *canyu*.... All for so little, Juan!"

"Señor not only has gold in bank but gold on his tongue.... It is indeed little you ask and little I risk."

Juan rode abreast of Vaughn and felt in his pockets for the checkbook and pencil, which he had neglected to return. Vaughn made of his face a grateful mask. This Mexican had become approachable, as Vaughn had known *canyu* would make him, but he was not yet under its influence to an extent which justified undue risk. Still, Vaughn decided, if the bandit freed his hands and gave him the slightest chance, he would jerk Juan out of that saddle. Vaughn did not lose sight of the fact that his feet would still be tied. He calculated exactly what he would do in case Juan's craftiness no longer possessed him. As the Mexican stopped his horse and reined in Vaughn's, the girl happened to turn round, as she often did, and she saw them. Vaughn caught a flash of big eyes and a white little face as Roseta vanished round a turn in the trail. Vaughn was glad for two things, that she had seen him stop and that she and her guard would be unable to see what was taking place.

All through these anxious moments of suspense Juan appeared to be studying the checkbook. If he could read English, it surely was only a few familiar words. The thought leaped to Vaughn's mind to write a note to the banker quite different from what he had intended. Most assuredly, if the El Paso banker ever saw that note Vaughn would be dead; and it was quite within the realm of possibility that it might fall into his hands.

"Señor, you may sign me the gold in your El Paso bank," said Juan, at length.

"Fine. You're a sensible man, Juan. But I cain't hold a pencil with my teeth."

The Mexican laughed. He was more amiable. Another hour and another few drinks of *canyu* would make him maudlin, devoid of quick wit or keen sight. A more favorable chance might befall Vaughn, and it might be wiser to wait. Surely on the ride ahead there would come a moment when he could act with lightning and deadly swiftness. But it would take iron will to hold his burning intent within bounds.

Juan kicked the horse Vaughn bestrode and moved him across the trail so that Vaughn's back was turned.

"There, señor," said the Mexican, and his lean dark hand slipped book and pencil into Vaughn's vest pocket.

The cunning beggar, thought Vaughn, in sickening disappointment! He had hoped Juan would free his bonds and then hand over the book. But Vaughn's ranger luck had not caught up with him yet.

He felt the Mexican tugging at the thongs around his wrists. They were tight—a fact to which Vaughn surely could attest. He heard him mutter a curse. Also he heard the short expulsion of breath—almost a pant—that betrayed the influence of the *canyu*.

"Juan, do you blame me for wanting those rawhides off my wrists?" asked Vaughn.

"Señor Medill is strong. It is nothing," returned the Mexican.

Suddenly the painful tension on Vaughn's wrists relaxed. He felt the thongs fall.

"Muchas gracias, señor!" he exclaimed. "Ahhh! . . . That feels good."

Vaughn brought his hands round in front to rub each swollen and discolored wrist. But all the time he was gathering his forces, like a tiger about to leap. Had the critical moment arrived?

"Juan, that was a little job to make a man rich—now wasn't it?" went on Vaughn pleasantly. And leisurely, but with every muscle taut, he turned to face the Mexican.

5

THE BANDIT WAS OUT OF REACH OF VAUGHN'S
eager hands. He sat back in the saddle
with an expression of interest on his
swarthy face. The ranger could not be
sure, but he would have gambled that
Juan did not suspect his deadly inten-
tions. Star was a mettlesome animal, but
Vaughn did not like the Mexican's horse,
to which he sat bound, and there were
several feet between them. If Vaughn had
been free to leap he might have, probably
would have, done so.

He swallowed his eagerness and began
to rub his wrists again. Presently he removed the pencil and book from his

pocket. It was not mere pretense that made it something of an effort to write out a check for Juan Mendoz for the three thousand and odd dollars that represented his balance in the El Paso bank.

"There, Juan. May some gringo treat your *chata* someday as you treat Señorita Uvaldo," said Vaughn, handing the check over to the Mexican.

"*Gracias*, señor," replied Juan, his black eyes upon the bit of colored paper. "Uvaldo's daughter then is your *chata*?"

"Yes. And I'll leave a curse upon you if she is mistreated."

"Ranger, I had my orders from Quinela. You would not have asked more."

"What has Quinela against Uvaldo?" asked Vaughn.

"They were *vaqueros* together years ago. But I don't know the reason for Quinela's hate. It is great and just. . . . Now, señor, the letter to your banker."

Vaughn tore a leaf out of his bankbook. On second thought he decided to write the letter in the bankbook, which would serve in itself to identify him. In case this letter ever was presented at the bank in El Paso he wanted it to mean something. Then it occurred to Vaughn to try out the Mexican. So he wrote a few lines.

"Read that, Juan," he said, handing over the book.

The man scanned the lines, which might as well have been written in Greek.

"Texas Medill does not write as well as he shoots," said Juan.

"Let me have the book. I can do better. I forgot something."

Receiving it back Vaughn tore out the page and wrote another.

Dear Mr. Jarvis:

If you ever see these lines you will know that I have been murdered by Quinela. Have the bearer arrested and wire to Captain Allerton, of the Rangers, at Brownsville. At this moment I am a prisoner of Juan Mendoz, lieutenant of Quinela. Miss Roseta Uvaldo is also a prisoner. She will be held for ransom and revenge. The place is in the hills somewhere east and south of Rock Ford trail.

MEDILL

Vaughn reading aloud to the Mexican improvised a letter which identified him, and cunningly made mention of the gold.

"Juan, isn't that better?" he said, as he handed the book back. "You'll do well not to show this to Quinela or anyone else. Go yourself *at once* to El Paso."

As Vaughn had expected the Mexican did not scan the letter. Placing the check in the bankbook he deposited it in an inside pocket of his tattered coat. Then without a word he drove Vaughn's horse forward on the trail, and following close behind soon came up with Roseta and her guard.

The girl looked back. Vaughn contrived, without making it obvious, to show her that his hands were free. A look of radiance crossed her wan face. The exertion and suspense had begun to tell markedly. Her form sagged in the saddle.

Juan appeared bent on making up for lost time, as he drove the horses forward at a trot. But this did not last long. Vaughn, looking at the ground, saw the black shadow of the Mexican as he raised the demijohn to his mouth to drink. What a sinister shadow! It forced Vaughn to think of what now should be his method of procedure. Sooner or later he was going to get his hand on his gun, which stuck out back of Juan's hip and hung down in its holster. That moment, when it came, would see the end of his captor. But Vaughn remembered how the horse he bestrode had bolted at the previous gunshot. He would risk more, shooting from the back of this horse than at the hands of the other Mexican. Vaughn's feet were tied in the stirrups with the rope passing underneath the horse. If he were thrown sideways out of the saddle it would be a perilous and very probably a fatal accident. He decided that at the critical time he would grip the horse with his legs so tightly that he could not be dislodged, and at that moment decide what to do about the other Mexican.

After Juan had a second drink, Vaughn slowly slackened the gait of his horse until Juan's mount came up to his horse's flank. Vaughn was careful to keep to the right of the trail. One glance at the Mexican's eyes sent a gush of hot blood over Vaughn. The effect of the *canyu* had been slow on this tough little man, but at last it was working.

"Juan, I'm powerful thirsty," said Vaughn.

"Señor, we come to water hole bimeby," replied the Mexican thickly.

"But won't you spare me a nip of *canyu*?"

"Our mescal drink is bad for gringos."

"I'll risk it, Juan. Just a nip. You're a good fellow and I like you. I'll tell Quinela how you had to fight your men back there,

163

when they wanted to kill me. I'll tell him Garcia provoked you. . . . Juan, you can see I may do you a turn."

Juan came up alongside Vaughn and halted. Vaughn reined his horse head and head with Juan's. The Mexican was sweating; his under lip hung a little; he sat loosely in his saddle. His eyes had lost their beady light and appeared to have filmed over.

Juan waited till the man ahead had turned another twist in the trail with Roseta. Then he lifted the obviously lightened demijohn from the saddlebag and extended it to Vaughn.

"A drop—señor," he said.

Vaughn pretended to drink. The hot stuff was like vitriol on his lips. He returned the jug, making a great show of the effect of the *canyu*, when as a matter of cold fact he was calculating distances. Almost he yielded to the temptation to lean and sweep a long arm forward. But a ranger could not afford to make mistakes. If Juan's horse had been a little closer! Vaughn expelled deeply his bated breath.

"Ah-h! Great stuff, Juan!" he exclaimed, and relaxed again.

They rode on, and Juan either forgot to drop behind or did not think it needful.

The trail was wide enough for two horses. Soon Roseta's bright red scarf burned against the gray-green brush again. She was looking back. So was her Mexican escort. And their horses were walking. Juan did not appear to take note of their slower progress. He long had passed the faculty for making minute observations. Presently he would take another swallow of *canyu*.

Vaughn began to talk, to express more gratitude to Juan, to dwell with flowery language on the effect of good drink—of which *canyu* was the sweetest and most potent in the world—of its power to make fatigue as if it were not, to alleviate pain and grief, to render the dreary desert of mesquite and stone a region of color and beauty and melody—even to resign a doomed ranger to his fate.

"Aye, señor—*canyu* is the blessed Virgin's gift to the peon," said Juan, and emphasized this tribute by having another generous drink.

They rode on. Vaughn asked only for another mile or two of lonely trail, free of interruption.

"How far, Juan?" asked Vaughn. "I cannot ride much farther with my feet tied under this horse."

"Till sunset—señor—which will be your last," replied the Mexican.

The sun was still high above the pipes of organ cactus. Two hours and more above the horizon! Juan could still speak intelligibly. It was in his lax figure and his sweating face, especially in the protruding eyeballs, that he betrayed the effect of the contents of the demijohn. After the physical letdown would come the mental slackening. That had already begun, for Juan was no longer alert.

They rode on, and Vaughn made a motion to Roseta that she must not turn to look back. Perhaps she interpreted it to mean more than it did, for she immediately began to engage her guard in conversation—something Vaughn had observed she had not done before. Soon the Mexican dropped back until his horse was walking beside Roseta's. He was a peon, and a heavy drink of *canyu* had addled the craft in his wits. Vaughn saw him bend down and loosen the rope that bound Roseta's left foot to the stirrup. Juan did not see this significant action. His gaze was fixed to the trail. He was singing:

"Ay, mía querida chata."

Roseta's guard took a long look back. Evidently Juan's posture struck him ap-

prehensively, yet did not wholly over-
come the interest that Roseta had
suddenly taken in him. When he gave her
a playful pat she returned it. He caught
her hand. Roseta did not pull very hard
to release it, and she gave him another
saucy little slap. He was reaching for her
when they passed out of Vaughn's sight
round a turn in the green-bordered trail.

Vaughn gradually and almost imperceptibly guided his horse closer to Juan.
At that moment a dog could be heard
barking in the distance. It did not make
any difference to Vaughn, except to ac-
centuate what had always been true—he
had no time to lose.

"Juan, the curse of *canyu* is that once
you taste it you must have more—or die,"
said Vaughn.

"It is—so—señor," replied the Mexican.

"You have plenty left. Will you let me
have one more little drink. . . . My last
drink of *canyu*, Juan! . . . I didn't tell you,
but it has been my ruin. My father was a
rich rancher. He disowned me because of
my evil habits. That's how I became a
ranger."

"Take it, señor. Your last drink," said
Juan.

Vaughn braced every nerve and fiber of
his being. He leaned a little. His left hand

went out—leisurely. But his eyes flashed like cold steel over the unsuspecting Mexican. Then, with the speed of a striking snake, his hand snatched the bone-handled gun from its sheath. Vaughn pulled the trigger. The hammer fell upon an empty chamber.

Juan turned. The gun crashed. *"Dios!"* he screamed in a strangled death cry.

The leaps of the horses were not quicker than Vaughn. He lunged to catch the Mexican—to keep him upright in the saddle. "Hold, Star!" he called sternly. "Hold!"

Star came down. But the other horse plunged and dragged him up the trail. Vaughn had his gun hand fast on the cantle and his other holding Juan upright. But for this grasp the frantic horse would have unseated him.

It was the ranger's job to manage both horses and look out for the other Mexican. He appeared on the trail riding fast, his carbine held high.

Vaughn let go of Juan and got the gun in his right hand. With the other then he grasped the Mexican's coat and held him straight in the saddle. He drooped himself over his pommel, to make it appear he had been the one shot. Meanwhile, he increased his iron leg grip on the horse he straddled. Star had halted and was being dragged.

The other Mexican came at a gallop, yelling. When he got within twenty paces Vaughn straightened up and shot him through the heart. He threw the carbine from him and pitching out of his saddle, went thudding to the ground. His horse bumped hard into the one Vaughn rode, and that was fortunate, for it checked the animal's first mad leap. In the melee that followed Juan fell off Star to be trampled under frantic hoofs. Vaughn hauled with all his might on the bridle. But he could not hold the horse and he feared that he would break the bridle. Bursting through the brush the horse ran wildly. What with his erratic flight and the low branches of mesquite, Vaughn had a hard job sticking on his back. Presently he got the horse under control and back onto the trail.

Some few rods down he saw Roseta, safe in her saddle, her head bowed with her hands covering her face. At sight of her Vaughn snapped out of the cold horror that had enveloped him.

"Roseta, it's all right. We're safe," he called eagerly as he reached her side.

"Oh, Vaughn!" she cried, lifting her convulsed and blanched face. "I knew you'd—kill them. . . . But, my God—how awful!"

"Brace up," he said sharply.

Then he got out his clasp knife and in a few slashes freed his feet from the stirrups. He leaped off the horse. His feet felt numb, as they had felt once when frozen.

Then he cut the ropes which bound Roseta's right foot to her stirrup. She swayed out of the saddle into his arms. Her eyes closed.

"It's no time to faint," he said sternly, carrying her off the trail, to set her on her feet.

"I—I won't," she whispered, her eyes opening, strained and dilated. "But hold me—just a moment."

Vaughn folded her in his arms, and the moment she asked was so sweet and precious that it almost overcame the will of a ranger in a desperate plight.

"Roseta—we're free, but not yet safe," he replied. "We're close to a hacienda— perhaps where Quinela is waiting. . . . Come now. We must get out of here."

Half carrying her, Vaughn hurried through the brush along the trail. The moment she could stand alone he whispered, "Wait here." And he ran onto the trail. He still held his gun. Star stood waiting, his head up. Both other horses had disappeared. Vaughn looked up and down the trail. Star whinnied. Vaughn hurried to bend over Juan. The Mexican lay on his face. Vaughn unbuckled the gun belt Juan had appropriated from him, and put it on. Next he secured his bankbook. Then he sheathed his gun. He grasped the bridle of Star and led him off the trail into the mesquite, back to where Roseta stood. She seemed all right now, only pale. But Vaughn avoided her eyes. The thing to do was to get away and not let sentiment deter him one instant. He mounted Star.

"Come, Roseta," he said. "Up behind me."

He swung her up and settled her in the saddle.

"There. Put your arms round me. Hold tight, for we're going to ride."

When she had complied, he grasped her left arm. At the same moment he heard voices up the trail and the rapid clipclop of hoofs. Roseta heard them, too. Vaughn felt her tremble.

"Don't fear, Roseta. Just you hang on. Here's where Star shines," whispered Vaughn, and guiding the nervous horse into the trail, he let him have a loose rein. Star did not need the shrill cries of the peons to spur him into action.

6

As the fleeing ranger sighted the peons, a babel of shrill voices arose. But no shots! In half a dozen jumps Star was going swift as the wind and in a moment a bend of the trail hid him from any possible marksman. Vaughn's concern for the girl behind him gradually eased.

At the end of a long straight stretch he looked back again. If *vaqueros* were riding in pursuit the situation would be serious. Not even Star could run away from a well-mounted cowboy of the Mexican haciendas. To his intense relief there was not one in sight. Nevertheless, he did not check Star.

"False alarm, Roseta," he said, craning his neck so he could see her face, pressed cheek against his shoulder. He was most marvelously aware of her close presence, but the realization did not impede him or Star in the least. She could ride. She had no stirrups, yet she kept her seat in the saddle.

"Let 'em come," she said, smiling up at him. Her face was pale, but it was not fear that he read in her eyes. It was fight.

Vaughn laughed in sheer surprise. He had not expected that, and it gave him such a thrill as he had never felt in his life before. He let go of Roseta's arm and took her hand where it clung to his coat. And he squeezed it with far more than reassurance. The answering pressure was unmistakable. A singular elation mounted in Vaughn's heart.

It did not, however, quite render him heedless. As Star turned a corner in the trail, Vaughn's keen glance saw that it was completely blocked by the same motley crew of big-sombreroed Mexicans and horses from which he had been separated not so long before that day.

"Hold tight!" he cried warningly to Roseta, as he swerved Star to the left. He drew his gun and fired two quick shots. He did not need to see that they took effect, for a wild cry arose, followed by angry yells.

Star beat the answering rifle shots into the brush. Vaughn heard the sing and twang of bullets. Crashing through the mesquites behind, added to the gunshots and lent wings to Star. This was a familiar situation to the great horse. Then for Vaughn it became a strenuous job to ride him, and a doubly fearful one, owing to Roseta. She clung like a broom to the speeding horse. Vaughn, after sheathing his gun, had to let go of her, for he needed one hand for the bridle and the other to ward off the whipping brush. Star made no allowance for that precious part of his burden at Vaughn's back, and he crashed through every opening between mesquites that presented itself. Vaughn dodged and ducked, but he never bent low enough for a branch to strike Roseta.

At every open spot in the mesquite, or long aisle between the cacti, Vaughn looked back to see if any of his pursuers were in sight. There was none, but he heard a horse pounding not far behind and to the right. And again he heard another on the other side. Holding the reins in his teeth Vaughn reloaded the gun. To be ready for snap shots he took advantage of every opportunity to peer on each side and behind him. But Star appeared gradually to be outdistancing his pursuers. The desert grew more open with a level gravel floor. Here Vaughn urged Star to his limit.

It became a dead run then, with the horse choosing the way. Vaughn risked less now from the stinging mesquite branches. The green wall flashed by on each side. He did not look back. While Star was at his best Vaughn wanted to get far enough ahead to slow down and save the horse. In an hour it would be dusk—too late for even a *vaquero* to track him until daylight had come again.

Roseta stuck like a leech, and the ranger had to add admiration to his other feelings toward her. Vaughn put his hand back to grasp and steady her. It did not take much time for the powerful strides of the horse to cover the miles. Finally Vaughn pulled him into a gallop and then into a lope.

"*Chata*, are you all right?" he asked, afraid to look back, after using that romantic epithet.

"Yes. But I can't—hold on—much longer," she panted. "If they catch us—shoot me first."

"Roseta, they will never catch us now," he promised.

"But—if they do—promise me," she entreated.

"I promise they'll never take us alive. But, child, keep up your nerve. It'll be sunset soon—and then dark. We'll get away sure."

"Vaughn, I'm not frightened. Only—I hate those people—and I mustn't fall—into their hands again. It means worse—than death."

"Hush! Save your breath," he replied, and wrapping a long arm backward round her slender waist he held her tight. "Come, Star, cut loose," he called, and dug the horse's flank with a heel.

Again they raced across the desert, this time in less of a straight line, though still to the north. The dry wind made tears dim Vaughn's eyes. He kept to open lanes and patches to avoid being struck by branches. And he spared Star only when he heard the animal's heaves of distress. Star was not easy to break from that headlong flight, but at length Vaughn got him down to a nervous walk. Then he let Roseta slip back into the saddle. His arm was numb from the long strain.

"We're—far ahead," he panted. "They'll trail—us till dark." He peered back across the yellow and green desert, slowly darkening in the sunset. "But we're safe—thank Gawd."

"Oh, what a glorious ride!" cried Roseta between breaths. "I felt that—even with death so close. . . . Vaughn, I'm such a little—fool. I longed—for excitement. Oh, I'm well punished. . . . But for you—"

"Save your breath, honey. We may need to run again. After dark you can rest and talk."

She said no more. Vaughn walked Star until the horse had regained his wind, and then urged him into a lope, which was his easiest gait.

The sun sank red in the west; twilight stole under the mesquite and the *palo verde*; dusk came upon its heels; the heat tempered and there was a slight breeze. When the stars came out Vaughn took his direction from them, and pushed on for several miles. A crescent moon, silver and slender, came up over the desert.

Young as it was, it helped brighten the open patches and the swales. Vaughn halted the tireless horse in a spot where a patch of grass caught the moonlight.

"We'll rest a bit," he said, sliding off, but still holding on to the girl. "Come."

She just fell off into his arms, and when he let her feet down she leaned against him. "Oh, Vaughn!" He held her a moment, sorely tempted. But he might take her weakness for something else.

"Can you stand? . . . You'd better walk around a little," he said.

"My legs are dead."

"I want to go back a few steps and listen. The night is still. I could hear horses at a long distance."

"Don't go far," she entreated him.

Vaughn went back where he could not hear the heaving, blowing horse, and turned his keen ear to the breeze. It blew gently from the south. Only a very faint rustle of leaves disturbed the desert silence. He held his breath and listened intensely. There was no sound! Even if he were trailed by a hound of a *vaquero* he was still far ahead. All he required now was a little rest for Star. He could carry the girl. On the way back across the open he tired to find the tracks Star had left. A man could trail them, but only on foot. Vaughn's last stern doubt took wing and vanished. He returned to Roseta.

"No sound. It is as I expected. Night has saved us," he said.

"Night and *canyu*. Oh, I watched you, ranger man."

"You helped, Roseta. That Mexican who led your horse was suspicious. But when you looked at him—he forgot. Small wonder . . . Have you stretched your legs?"

"I tried. I walked some, then flopped here. . . . Oh, I want to rest and sleep."

"I don't know about your sleeping, but you can rest riding," he replied, and removing his coat folded it around the pommel of his saddle, making a flat seat there. Star was munching the grass. He was already fit for another race. Vaughn saw to the cinches, and then mounted again, and folded the sleeves of his coat up over the pommel. "Give me your hand. . . . Put your foot in the stirrup. Now." He caught her and lifted her in front of him, and settling her comfortably upon the improvised seat, he put his left arm around her. Many a wounded comrade had he packed this way. "How is—that?" he asked unsteadily.

"It's very nice," she replied, her dark eyes looking inscrutable in the moonlight. And she relaxed against his arm and shoulder.

Vaughn headed Star north at a brisk walk. He could not be more than six hours from the river in a straight line. Canyons and rough going might deter him. But even so he could make the Rio Grande before dawn. Then and then only did he surrender to the astonishing presence of

Roseta Uvaldo, to the indubitable fact that he had saved her, and then to thoughts wild and whirling of the future. He gazed down upon the oval face so blanched in the moonlight, into the staring black eyes whose look might mean anything.

"Vaughn, was it that guard or you—who called me *chata*?" she asked, dreamily.

"It was I—who dared," he replied huskily.

"Dared! Then you were not just carried away—for the moment?"

"No, Roseta. . . . I confess I was as—as bold as that poor devil."

"Vaughn, do you know what *chata* means?" she asked gravely.

"It is the name a *vaquero* has for his sweetheart."

"You mean it, señor?" she asked imperiously.

"Lord help me, Roseta, I did, and I do. . . . I've loved you long."

"But you never told me!" she exclaimed, with wonder and reproach. "Why?"

"What hope had I? A poor ranger. Texas Medill! . . . Didn't you call me 'killer of Mexicans'?"

"I reckon I did. And it is because you

are that I'm alive to thank God for it. . . . Vaughn, I always liked you, respected you as one of Texas' great rangers—feared you, too. I never knew my real feelings. . . . But I—I love you *now.*"

The night wore on, with the moon going down, weird and coldly bright against the dark vaulted sky. Roseta lay asleep in Vaughn's arm. For hours he had gazed, after peering ahead and behind, always vigilant, always the ranger, on that wan face against his shoulder. The silent moonlit night, the lonely ride, the ghastly forms of cactus were real, though Vaughn never trusted his senses there. This was only the dream of the ranger. Yet the sweet fire of Roseta's kisses still lingered on his lips.

At length he changed her again from his right arm back to his left. And she awakened, but not fully. In all the years of his ranger service, so much of which he lived over on this ride, there had been nothing to compare with this. For his reward had been exalting. His longings had received magnificent fulfillment. His duty had not been to selfish and unappreciative officials, but to a great state—to its people— to the native soil upon which he had been born. And that hard duty, so poorly recompensed, so bloody and harrowing at times, had by some enchantment bestowed upon one ranger at least a beautiful girl of the border, frankly and honestly Texan, yet part Spanish, retaining something of the fire and spirit of the Dons who had once called Texas their domain.

In the gray of dawn, Vaughn lifted Roseta down from the weary horse upon the south bank of the Rio Grande.

"We are here, Roseta," he said gladly. "It will soon be light enough to ford the river. Star came out just below Brownsville. There's a horse, Roseta! He shall never be risked again. . . . In an hour you will be home."

"Home? Oh, how good! . . . But what shall I say, Vaughn?" she replied, evidently awakening to the facts of her predicament.

"Dear, who was the feller you ran—rode off with yesterday mawnin'?" he asked.

"Didn't I tell you?" And she laughed. "It happened to be Elmer Wade—*that* morning. . . . Oh, he was the unlucky one. The bandits beat him with quirts, dragged him off his horse. Then they led me away and I didn't see him again."

Vaughn had no desire to acquaint her then with the tragic fate that had overtaken that young man.

"You were not—elopin'?"

"*Vaughn!* It was only fun."

"Uvaldo thinks you eloped. He was wild. He raved."

"The devil he did!" exclaimed Roseta rebelliously. "Vaughn, what did *you* think?"

"Dearest, I—I was only concerned with trackin' you," he replied, and even in the gray gloom of the dawn those big dark eyes made his heart beat faster.

"Vaughn, I have peon blood in me," she said, and she might have been a princess for the pride with which she confessed it. "My father always feared I'd run true to the Indian. Are you afraid of your *chata*?"

"No, darlin'."

"Then I shall punish Uvaldo. . . . I shall elope."

"Roseta!" cried Vaughn.

"Listen." She put her arms around his neck, and that was a long reach for her. "Will you give up the ranger service? I— I couldn't bear it, Vaughn. You have earned release from the service all Texans are so proud of."

"Yes, Roseta. I'll resign," he replied

with boyish, eager shyness. "I've some money—enough to buy a ranch."

"Far from the border?" she entreated.

"Yes, far. I know just the valley—way north, under the *Llano Estacado*. . . . But, Roseta, I shall have to pack a gun—till I'm forgotten."

"Very well, I'll not be afraid—way north," she replied. Then her sweet gravity changed to mischief. "We will punish Father. Vaughn, we'll elope right now! We'll cross the river—get married—and drive out home to breakfast. . . . How Dad will rave! But he would have me elope, though he'd never guess I'd choose a ranger."

Vaughn swung her up on Star, and leaned close to peer up at her, to find one more assurance of the joy that had befallen him. He was not conscious of asking, when she bent her head to bestow kisses upon his lips.

HISTORICAL NOVELS
OF THE AMERICAN FRONTIERS

DON WRIGHT

☐ 58991-2   THE CAPTIVES $4.50
☐ 58992-0   Canada $5.50

☐ 58989-0   THE WOODSMAN $3.95
☐ 58990-4   Canada $4.95

DOUGLAS C. JONES

☐ 58459-7   THE BAREFOOT BRIGADE $4.50
☐ 58460-0   Canada $5.50

☐ 58457-0   ELKHORN TAVERN $4.50
☐ 58458-9   Canada $5.50

☐ 58453-8   GONE THE DREAMS AND DANCING $3.95
               (Winner of the Golden Spur Award)
☐ 58454-6   Canada $4.95

☐ 58450-3   SEASON OF YELLOW LEAF $3.95
☐ 58451-1   Canada $4.95

EARL MURRAY

☐ 58596-8   HIGH FREEDOM $4.95
☐ 58597-6   Canada   5.95

Buy them at your local bookstore or use this handy coupon:
Clip and mail this page with your order.

Publishers Book and Audio Mailing Service
P.O. Box 120159, Staten Island, NY 10312-0004

Please send me the book(s) I have checked above. I am enclosing $_____
(please add $1.25 for the first book, and $.25 for each additional book to
cover postage and handling. Send check or money order only—no CODs.)

Name _____

Address _____

City _____ State/Zip _____

Please allow six weeks for delivery. Prices subject to change without notice.

MORE
HISTORICAL NOVELS
OF THE AMERICAN FRONTIERS

<u>JOHN BYRNE COOK</u>

THE SNOWBLIND MOON TRILOGY
(Winner of the Golden Spur Award)

☐ 58150-4　BETWEEN THE WORLDS　　　　　$3.95
☐ 58151-2　　　　　　　　　　　　Canada $4.95

☐ 58152-0　THE PIPE CARRIERS　　　　　$3.95
☐ 58153-9　　　　　　　　　　　　Canada $4.95

☐ 58154-7　HOOP OF THE NATION　　　　$3.95
☐ 58155-5　　　　　　　　　　　　Canada $4.95

<u>W. MICHAEL GEAR</u>

☐ 58304-3　LONG RIDE HOME　　　　　　$3.95
☐ 58305-1　　　　　　　　　　　　Canada $4.95

<u>JOHN A. SANDFORD</u>

☐ 58843-6　SONG OF THE MEADOWLARK　$3.95
☐ 58844-4　　　　　　　　　　　　Canada $4.95

<u>JORY SHERMAN</u>

☐ 58873-8　SONG OF THE CHEYENNE　　$2.95
☐ 58874-6　　　　　　　　　　　　Canada $3.95

☐ 58871-1　WINTER OF THE WOLF　　　$3.95
☐ 58872-X　　　　　　　　　　　　Canada $4.95

Buy them at your local bookstore or use this handy coupon:
Clip and mail this page with your order.

Publishers Book and Audio Mailing Service
P.O. Box 120159, Staten Island, NY 10312-0004

Please send me the book(s) I have checked above. I am enclosing $_____
(please add $1.25 for the first book, and $.25 for each additional book to
cover postage and handling. Send check or money order only—no CODs.)

Name _____

Address _____

City _____State/Zip _____

Please allow six weeks for delivery. Prices subject to change without notice.

BESTSELLING BOOKS FROM TOR
